Anna Noyes is a recent graduate of the Iowa Writers'
Workshop. Her fiction has appeared in *VICE*, *A Public
Space*, and *Guernica*, amongst others. She has received
the Aspen Words Emerging Writer Fellowship and the
James Merrill House Fellowship. *Goodnight, Beautiful
Women* received the 2013 Henfield Prize for Fiction.

GOODNIGHT, BEAUTIFUL WOMEN

Stories

Anna Noyes

Atlantic Books
London

First published in 2016 in the United States of America by Grove Press, and imprint of Grove Atlantic.

First published in hardback and e-book in Great Britain in 2016 by Atlantic Books, an imprint of Atlantic Books Ltd.

"Treelaw" originally appeared in *A Public Space*, 2015
"Werewolf" originally appeared in *Vice*, 2013
"Hibernation" originally appeared in *FiveChapters* and *Summer Stories: Paintings by Leslie Anderson, Stories by Ten Maine Writers* published by Shanti Arts Publishing, 2013

1 2 3 4 5 6 7 8 9 10

A CIP catalogue record for this book is available from the British Library.

Hardback ISBN: 9781786490674
Trade paperback ISBN: 9781786490391
E-book ISBN: 9781786490407

Printed and bound by CPI Group (UK) Ltd, Croydon, CR0 4YY

Atlantic Books
An Imprint of Atlantic Books Ltd
Ormond House
26–27 Boswell Street
London
WC1N 3JZ

www.atlantic-books.co.uk

For my beautiful mom

Contents

Hibernation

Joni called the sheriff right after it happened. Her voice was clear and steady, and the line she gave was the right one. *I believe my husband has drowned in the quarry by our house.* She changed out of Jack's boxers into jeans and a gray button-up. It was difficult picking out appropriate clothing for a woman who'd just lost her husband. She combed her hair until it sparked with static. Joni, who once cried over a Folgers Coffee commercial, hadn't cried yet. This frustrated her, like a sneeze that wouldn't come. She tucked some tissues up her sleeve, just in case.

Joni told it to the sheriff like it was. "I wake up in the middle of the night to the sound of my name from outside. Probably around one in the morning. I look out the window by the bed and Jack's wading into the quarry, holding a small hunk of granite. He was wearing a white T-shirt, so I could

1

see him clearly, and I saw his head go under. By the time I got outside, he was gone."

The sheriff asked her questions, glancing up at the appropriate moments with a look of sympathy. "Did he give any indication he might do something like this?" he said.

"There were signs," said Joni.

He looked toward the window that faced the water. "Wish we could dredge it like a lake," he said. "Depending how far a person swam beyond the shallow ledge, and if he weighed himself down, a body could be trapped in a crevice. We'll get divers out tomorrow, if he doesn't show up. Quarry's can be tricky to search, though. Deep, murky, a lot of junk down there. We might have to drain it some. May I be frank?"

"Of course," she said.

"There'll be a thorough investigation. We'll run a missing persons report. Take every measure. But this sounds like a suicide." He paused for her reaction, scanning her face, which she let drop into her hands. He patted her shoulder twice.

"Excuse me," she said, looking at the floor between the spread of her fingers. She tried to think of heartbreaking things as she rooted for the tissue. It had traveled up her sleeve, now a lump by her elbow. That movie where hoodlums kick an old homeless man to death. Footage of cows lowing, wild eyed, on their way to slaughter.

After he left she stood at the window. When she realized who she was looking for she gave a little laugh. There was a smear on the glass where her nose had pressed.

Jack was in the quarry, and he had drowned. He was dead. The other possibilities made her hands start to shake. Jack let Joni watch him go into the quarry, and go under, but he swam to the other side and snuck through the woods. From there he found a new life with a different woman. Another scenario, the most paranoid but not out of the question, was that Jack walked into the water, climbed out on the other side, and was in the woods. He was watching Joni from outside, watching everything she did, because he was testing her. He was trying to see how she would behave when he was gone. If she would fail him.

Jack had been hell-bent for the quarry for a long time. That he was in there seemed to Joni like a brief stage in his life cycle, a necessary hibernation.

Joni knew she was OK, even if her thinking wasn't. She had clean hair. No salt spilled on her counter and there were no maggots in her trash cans. She had a fruit bowl filled with nectarines, and a row of books on the shelf arranged from large to small.

But she misspoke at the post office. She couldn't help it. She was talking to a woman who was in town for Labor Day weekend. The woman's French Bulldog was peeing on the wheelchair ramp. Jack had been gone for two weeks, his body never recovered. Other policemen came and went, asking her questions, looking at her sidelong. And then the suicide was official. And this woman gave Joni a look of pitying concern, and was hugging her, and Joni said thank you, but we can't be sure now. Nothing is definite. I'm trying not to give up hope that he'll come home soon. *That he'll come home soon.* That was it, she guessed; the tripwire that made gossip of her strange behavior blast through town.

The trouble with Jack began with little things. Joni put her hand on his neck during dinner and he pulled away. He told her that it was payback for the time she didn't look up when he touched his foot to hers under the table. And then he started counting on his fingers, biting his tongue as he struggled to recall infractions. He counted when she did something wrong, like not lifting the lid on the pot of whatever he was cooking to smell it and taste a bite, or turning away from him in bed to face the wall, even though that's the only way she could lie comfortably.

One afternoon he showed up during recess at the school where she taught. A crowd was gathered at the jungle gym dome, and there was Jack hanging upside down at the top. He yelled to her in a voice that carried across the playground, "I thought I'd come visit you. You never take off work to visit me. You never surprise me in the studio." The other teacher on duty blew the whistle, and Joni hiked her skirt and climbed over a rung to be in there with him. He stayed hanging upside down and said, "You have to kiss me now, Teach. Since I came out all this way."

The awful thing was how his face looked, with the blood rushing into his forehead. His blond hair was a wild beard. His eyes curved down at the corners. He was waiting for her to kiss him, but his mouth looked like a toothy frown. She didn't want to get near him. When he finally flipped

4

back down he was counting. He gave her a long stare, then headed for his car.

"I'm coming with you," she yelled after him. When she asked the principal for the rest of the day off, he warned her that the next time her private life interfered with her work life she would be let go. By the time she got her things from the lounge, Jack was pulling out of the lot. Joni jogged after him. She could hear his muffler as he slowed through the curves away from her.

At bedtime she curls around the space that used to be Jack. She holds her hand above the shallow depression from his head, careful not to touch the pillowcase. As she changes into her pajamas she thinks of what someone spying through the window would see: the darkened gears of her spine, her long red hair down her back the way Jack liked it. Sleep is no good. She leaves bed to microwave milk with honey and cinnamon. On the way to the kitchen, she realizes she's running, and slows herself. Moths thrum against the screen as she closes the kitchen window.

Back under the covers she bites the edge of the mug to stop her teeth from chattering. The night hums with the sound of her pumping blood. When she turns on the fan, there is the promise of what she cannot hear. For example, Jack gasping for air as he breaks the surface of the water, or the wet flop of his steps across the porch as he comes back home.

"Honey Bunny," she prays, sitting up in bed. She prays to the hot milk sweetened with honey that her mother used to make her on nights she couldn't sleep. "Honey Bunny, Honey Bunny," says Joni, but then she has to laugh at herself. She has been praying like this for the past week.

"I think Jack's still alive," she'd told her sister, who had just gotten back to New Jersey from the funeral, over the phone.

"Oh?" said her sister. Joni could hear baby's laughter in the background. Her niece.

"Mop mop mop," said the baby.

"Oh?" her sister said again. There was a long pause, the clatter of plates. "Sweetie, you need to pray."

"Prayer won't bring him back home," said Joni.

"No, you need to pray for yourself."

"I wouldn't know who to pray to," Joni said. "I don't believe there's anyone to pray to. And I wouldn't know what to say."

"Call it whatever you want," said her sister. "Just give the thing a name." The sounds of a home rattled on in the background.

Joni has been cycling through names. The prayer won't come, but she can make a list of gods, saying them aloud like she's giving roll call. Honey Bunny, please. Please, Abraham Lincoln. Merlin. David Byrne. In the morning the sheets smell like soup from her sweat. Her mouth tastes like pennies.

Dawn. Joni's footsteps mark the wet grass as she walks to the quarry. She swallows the last of her morning tea, then throws the mug toward the dark slab of water and watches it disappear below the black surface. She lies down on her stomach and scoots closer to the edge, fear tangled in her throat like fishing line. *Crazy,* she thinks, how she's afraid he will pull her in.

Jack had started to throw things into the quarry. That was when she understood something was really wrong.

In the beginning, Joni only felt good around Jack. She sped home from school, her pulse beating between her thighs. His Toyota, the letters repainted to spell Coyote, was parked with its plow pressed to a melting snow bank. She stood outside and watched him through the garage window, the drill whining against his sculpture. How nice to watch Jack from a distance, listening to the wet landing of flakes on her raincoat's hood. When he came out to join her, she wiped the rock dust from his eyebrows. His body tasted like chalk, same as the smell that lingered on her hands after long lessons at the blackboard. The snow turned to rain, and the woods had a sweetfern smell that meant spring was coming. His mouth was warm, his cold hand pressing down her jeans. He pulled her into the bed of the truck, spread out his coat and Joni lay back and propped her leg against the cool of the wheel well. And finally, after the whole day of thinking on it, she guided him inside her. She felt like scattered iron filings, and Jack was the magnet that pulled them together.

A rusted Ford emerges from the woods and parks at a cliff across the quarry. It sputters black smoke out the back. Two men climb out. They push the truck straight into the water. She imagines the leaky plume of oils as the truck falls, the blink of headlights and the grinding halt of the motor. The water bubbles where the truck went under.

The men strip naked and jump into the quarry, hooting at the cold. She's heard stories that the quarry is used as a junkyard, and that dirty people wash there, but she hasn't seen it. It doesn't scare her to see it, really. Just old men soaping their beards in the green morning light.

Joni puts her cheek to the mottled granite. She feels almost comfortable with the men swimming in the distance. She hasn't been sleeping, and she curls up, her breath slow, her body heavy, and then she's sinking down into the quarry. The water is green and backlit. When she touches ground, two plumes of silt rise like ink around her. She stands inside a circle of cars, their wheel wells silky with green moss. She steps around the beer cans that are wedged into the mud. The abandoned backhoes are tall as trees. The cars' hoods are caved, their windows webbed with cracks. The bodies waver by in Joni's periphery. She can just sense the glow of their skin, paled from living so many miles out of the sun. *Better lie down,* she thinks, *keep low to the ground.* The quarry mud gives beneath her weight. The map of algae trawls for her sleeping body. It finds and covers her over. How silent the dream is, what a nice place to get some sleep.

In the beginning the sweet taste inside Jack's mouth was the most surprising. She recognized him as something she'd always known but just realized, like cleaning out her mother's dresser after her funeral and finding the pine pillow she used to scent her clothes. Joni had never placed her mother's smell as pine. It was so fiercely known to her, and forgotten. She'd dug her nails into the pillow and sobbed.

It took years for Jack to learn her inventory: the freckle on the middle knuckle of her left hand, the one on the ridge of her right ear, the white scar on her eyelid that she got from playing capture the flag in the woods when she was twelve, the three stretch marks across each hip, the scar inside her belly button where they'd inserted the camera to look for an ovarian tumor, the two chalk scars under her pubic hair from the surgery that removed a benign cyst. He'd put his tongue in her belly button, years healed, very gently, and how good it felt. Only he would know about that place.

When she goes inside at nightfall, the path lights are off even though she left them on. Moonlight. The quarry is moving into the air around her, the woods are humming with frogs and night noise. She opens the back door. Of course, of course, the kitchen floor is wet, the bathroom floor is wet, there are watermarks along the shelves where she keeps Jack's favorite granola and his nighttime tea, there are two damp fingerprints on the paper towel roll, and a trail leading back out onto the porch where she won't look. She flips on every switch in the house, lighting the living room, the front hallway, illuminating the bare bulbs in the bathroom and the kitchen. The whole moonlit scene outside disappears and in the bedroom, where there are eight windows side-by-side looking out at the quarry, all she can see is her reflection, eight times over. The mouth hangs open. The eyes appraise her.

Before he left Jack brought home sage, bound with yellow string. He said he needed to smudge the house. He said it was cleansing, a Native American ritual that drove away bad energy and bad spirits. He went to each corner of their cabin and let the smoke wash over the surfaces to clear away all of their impurities. He smudged her makeup case and the plunger that was pushed behind the toilet tank, stood on a stool to get at the rafters, and crawled on his hands and knees to cleanse under the bed. Then he drew the smoke in an oval around her body until her eyes were stinging. When she thought he was done, he moved up to her face, and started making the shape of a figure eight. She laughed.

He went into the bathroom, where he put out the ember in the glass Joni used to rinse her mouth of toothpaste. "Sixteen," he said solemnly, ticking his fingers against the air. "Sixteen times and it's only Wednesday."

Joni gets in the shower and prays. One stream of water is stronger than the others and she aligns it with her backbone, bending so the stream shoots hard against each knob. These days naked she feels all head, where the thoughts are whirring. It is a burden to soap and carry this creature body, all of its many parts. Coccyx, tailbone, scapula.

The next morning there are ants. When she wakes up there is one on her cheek, one floating in a teacup on the bedside table, and then there are more crawling out of the walls every minute longer that Joni looks, tooling along with their feelers twitching up and down.

In town they tell her that ants like to nest in homes where the wood is rotting. They sell her something to kill them, and when she asks how it works they describe ants' love for sugar. The poison tastes like sugar to them, and it smells like sugar, when they pass their feelers over it. They will carry it, the poison twice their size, back to their nest and give it to their babies, as a nice thing to eat. That is how it kills them all. She buys ten traps and puts them in all the rooms.

When Joni swings her feet out of bed there are piles of crisp ant bodies on the floor. There are small graveyards in the corner of every room. There is a horror show of ants drowning in the toilet. For a moment she thinks, *Oh no, they got into the rice somehow, they've carried it all over the house,* but then she realizes it's the babies, wrapped in thin white eggs the size of rice, with a surface that folds when she presses it with the sole of her slipper. The ants were rushing to carry the eggs from the nest, emergency evacuation, before the poison slowed them.

Jack had come running in one afternoon while she was shelling peas at the kitchen table and said, "I got rid of the silverware last night. I dumped it in the quarry. It's giving us something. It has a bad energy." She kept on shelling peas until a few rolled off the table. That night when she went to make lamb for dinner all the knives were gone. The tool for basting and the grate to let the juices drip down from the meat, gone. Jack was in the shower. As he toweled off she hugged him from behind, pressed her chest against his back for warmth.

"I don't know what's happening to me," he said, and she kissed his ear.

"That's OK. I know you," Joni said. "I have always known you, I will always know you."

"But something's gotten into me. Something in this house has turned. It's toxic. I don't know why I feel this way."

Joni put her hand to his chest, over his port-wine stain, a pink flush that had been there since birth. She thought about the white star inside her belly button, plus all the stories she had told him, vignettes to equal her life, to take him back to the very beginning. How the caul stayed intact during her mother's labor, and she was born inside the watery sack. Joni had told him all her stories worth telling. She had been known.

That night she looked out the window to see Jack standing at the edge of the quarry, skipping their white dish set, a wedding present from her sister, across the water. The plates glowed as they skimmed the surface, giant flat stones. Her sister splurged for the whole set, the salad plates, dessert plates, china teacups that felt too frail in Joni's hands. Off it went.

The next day she had driven to the grocery store and walked up and down the home wares aisle. She bought plastic utensils, paper plates, and Dixie cups; a candle for the kitchen that was supposed to smell like apple pie, and one for the bedroom that smelled like fresh laundry, how homes were supposed to smell. When she got back there was a gap next to the stove. Their refrigerator was gone. In its place, an outline of dust balls and two words from the magnetic poetry that had been up on its door for years. She knew the sentence-long poems by heart. *Tall teacher who dug winter,* Jack had written for her. *Slow world, color came in pools of green. Four o'clock and white morning glow. Fat balloon cat. Wet dream. She's sad and crackly.*

Joni got in bed. Outside Jack was dragging a sculpture toward the quarry on a blanket. The glass-smooth granite caught the light where he'd worn it down. She did nothing to stop him. She watched him haul sculptures from his studio to the quarry, dumping all of his work into the water, until the sun went down.

"Something here is making me sick," he told her when he came inside, and Joni pretended she was sleeping. When he cried noiselessly, covering his head with the pillow that smelled like him, she did not hold him. And when she fell asleep, she dreamed that Jack turned into a creature that lived in the water. He broke the surface, came at her across the lawn, and she took a pistol from behind her back. Her bullets made his body dance.

When she'd started awake, the empty space beside her vibrated with Jack's absence, present but invisible, like un-stirred phosphorescence. She couldn't look because she knew he was outside waiting for her, watching from the other side of the window screen. Watching her run a hand through her hair, rub the inside corners of her eyes, check the numbers on the clock. She heard his splashing steps into the water, knew without looking about the wake he left through the yellow surface scum. Then she did look out the window, to see what she had known she would, the last of his head before he dipped below.

Perhaps they could get the divers back to search for him again. They could find his body. Joni could grieve under the comforter and preheat the oven for meals for one. She'd sit up in bed to eat. The quarry would be covered with wet yellow leaves. The quarry would freeze over. She would plant green beans in the spring, and eat them topped with salt, pepper, and thick pats of butter.

Maybe the poison was already inside him the night they met, at a friend's wedding. Jack stole a case of pink champagne from the caterer's truck. He was filled with the tiny bubbles by the time he found her in the kitchen. She was sitting on the counter, surrounded by buckets of lobster shells, eating a lime. She told him her feet were bruised from so much dancing, and he got down on his knees and slipped off one grass-stained shoe, and then the other. She made him drink some milk. They danced in the kitchen. His hand crushed the Baby's Breath tucked behind her ear. She moved him inside her hips and they kissed in the coat closet against the crash of wire hangers. In the bed she pushed his briefs down with her feet. He undressed her for hours. He just couldn't get his fingers around the buttons.

Maybe whatever it was that took Jack was already there, incubating.

Joni gets out of bed. It's three in the morning. She pulls the sheet up neatly to the pillow, tucks it back. Opens the door. No one is out there waiting for her. The granite is cold on her bare feet. She lifts the nightgown over her head and leaves it folded on the rock. Tests the water with her toe. As she wades out over the shallow outcropping, the stone underfoot grows slick with algae. She is up to her hips now, and she crouches down, letting her feet teeter on the ledge before pushing off into deep water. She is a bad swimmer, not sure and straight or with a sense of breath, but moving with just enough effort to stay afloat, and she swims out, trying to ignore the plunge beneath her. The house is glowing in her periphery, and she sees a pale woman inside, the flash of red hair moving through the bedroom. A blur that's gone when she stares. The fear is tangible, pulsating, radiant on her skin.

Deep down, the soft world of the quarry stirs. The only noise underwater is the churning of Joni's legs, keeping her afloat. And then she is on her back, a bright cutout against the surface: strong arms and legs, full hips, long neck, hair tangled and weightless. The water's many hands swim up and hold her, pressing her body to the sky.

Treelaw

At O'Connor's store today everyone, even the Coffee Brandy crowd in the back room, especially them, seemed to know Dad was dead. In a place like Treelaw, you can't keep anything to yourself. Dollie O'Connor leaned over the counter to make her loud, phlegmy apologies, then peered down at my kid to say, "I hope you have it better than your folks, little lady. Don't you throw out your life like Granddad did." Kimmy's three and just learning it's polite to shake hands, so she stuck out her hand, red from the Fla-Vor-Ice we shared in the car.

"Isn't she cunning?" said Dollie. She said it like the words were something sour to spit out. Kimmy hid her face in my skirt, her breath hot against my leg. I was thinking all babies are mouth breathers. I was thinking too that Dollie is a cunt. Everyone knows about the six-inch scar she gave her

17

ex-boyfriend when she pushed him into scrap metal, and that there's only one bruised peach for sale because she spent the store money on pills. It's no secret Dollie snuck by a neighbor's trailer when her boyfriend was sleeping around and killed all the neighbor's chickens and a pig.

But I didn't feel the need to air this out in the middle of the store. Dollie totaled me up and I was short, so instead of making any kind of scene I put Kimmy's whoopie pie back, thinking a skinny kid's got enough problems, then changed my mind and had Dollie strike the charge for Drill's Roulette Riches scratch card. The register went haywire and spit out a long, white slip, and that's when the bell above the door dinged and Mandy walked in. I knew her before she looked up—dirty blonde curls, circles under her eyes just like Grace, long legs. When she spotted me I looked quickly away so we had a chance to pretend we didn't recognize each other. I could feel heat move from my cheeks to my ears and my right eye starting to wander like it did when I lied.

"Hey," she said softly, and I thought, *This is it, she'll call me out in front of Dollie and the line crowding behind me, in front of Kimmy who has her mouth full of whoopie pie.* But Mandy just put her arms around me.

"I'm so sorry about your dad," she said against my neck.

There wasn't a thing I could think that would be good enough to say.

"How's life?" I said. "How's your mom?"

"Oh, you know, school. Mom's OK. Not great." She pulled back to look at me, and she looked at me long and hard.

Balancing my bag on one arm, I grabbed Kimmy's sticky hand. "Hey, meet my kid. Kimmy, say hi to Mandy." She stared at Mandy from behind my legs and didn't say anything or smile.

"She looks just like you," Mandy said.

A part of me was happy because Kimmy was mine and loved me and would forget Mandy as soon as we got out of the store.

"Well, I'll let you two go," Mandy said. "You're my family. You're both my family, no matter what."

"Bye," said Kimmy.

I told her she was a good, polite girl. She clung to my legs as we backed out the door, so synchronized we didn't trip.

As soon as we were outside Kimmy started crying, but she didn't seem to know why.

I once saw a birth on television where the mom labored in a bath, and all her friends and her mom were around her. The baby was born underwater, calm, and it floated and held its breath right off. That's how I pictured Kimmy being born, Grace and Mandy with me, even though of course it couldn't be like that.

Kimmy was born with just Drill at the hospital. He spent the labor flipping through this Toyota engine manual to see if he couldn't fix up that free car he'd got down in Augusta, and wouldn't the baby like a new car. The drugs made my vision blurry, and when they put her on my chest I couldn't focus on her face.

How I was conceived, Dad always said, was my mom got caught smuggling pills from Canada. He told me she quit her birth control soon after so the judge might pity the pregnant lady. I wanted to know her better than just this story and used to steal her photo from Dad's drawer. It was black and white. In it she was leaning back against a tree. She wore a cropped shirt that showed her belly button. She was stabbed in prison, and she died from the wound. I wondered where on her body, and why. In the picture she had nice teeth.

Dad said he took the picture, but I don't believe it, the way she's looking at the camera. My guess is she hated him. My guess is she was looking at me, even if she didn't know it. Like she knew I'd spend all night lying with my dog on the carpet that Dad's shuffling had worn down to something hard and slippery, looking back at her.

Dad was a wormer his whole life. He was also a sternman, and between seasons lay in bed, a bowl of thawed clams on his belly for snacking, another bowl on his legs for the shells.

We lived together on the street Dad grew up on, the same street where three of his sisters lived. Two of them wouldn't talk to Dad, and the aunt that stayed friendly told me he only saved me from foster care for the welfare checks, but anyways he stopped getting money when I was nine and didn't send me back into care, so that couldn't have been the whole truth. That's how it's always been in this town, people saying shitty things to try and turn normal people into monsters. Dad only touched me twice. Both times he was gentle and looked bewildered, like my body wasn't the one he expected, but it was too late, too embarrassing for us both, to turn back.

The first time I ever talked to Grace she didn't ask why I was calling so late on a school night, just said, "Hold on, sweetie," and woke Mandy up. Mandy and me did show choir at school together. I felt like I had to say something big so I told her Dad punched out all the windows in the boathouse, which he had done, just not that night, but the field was still shiny with glass so the story seemed real enough.

Before Grace and Mandy pulled into Dad's drive they cut their headlights. I sprinted to the car and Mandy and I sank low in the backseat and shrieked, full of the thrill of the kidnapping. We peeked at the bonfire going in Fulton's lot, sparks hissing off a burning couch, and I recognized my cousin swaying topless by the fire.

The streets in Alma were quiet and moonlit. Their house stood all by itself at the end of a paved drive, with lawns on either side. The path to their doorstep was lined with lamps that ran off stored-up sunshine. Behind the house waves crashed on the beach. In Treelaw I'd have to walk two miles to the wharf if I wanted the water. The rooms were bright with lamps and vases of cut flowers and furniture that looked like it should be roped off, like it wasn't safe to touch. Their two white cats rubbed against my sneakers. My bed was tucked under the slanted ceiling in Mandy's bedroom. It was like sleeping in a boat's cabin, and I could stay as long as I needed. Bronze and gold animal figurines lined the windowsill that looked out on the ocean. I rearranged them.

I remember Grace giving her name to the Alma pool attendant, then saying "and my daughters," each time me thinking they'd catch her in the lie. I stood behind Mandy, with her pale hair and bikini same as Grace, in my gym shorts and T-shirt, trying to hide my face.

Mandy and I dedicated love songs over the radio to boys from school. My voice, when it played through the speakers, sounded like a stranger's—husky and shy and older. I wanted to block my ears. We practiced slow dancing with each other.

At night, with Grace, we often walked down the wide, empty road to the lamplight at the end of the pier and watched the water for bloodworms, which Mandy and Grace thought were eels, and I didn't tell them the difference. My dad called the worms dimes, because they sold at ten cents each, barely worth him bending down for. I pictured the worms as dimes, silver and quick, hard to tell apart from the light on the water.

It didn't take two trips home to empty out my half of the dresser and pack my deodorant and eye makeup and slippers into a garbage bag. Dad had piled beaver hides all over my bed. He was saving up to sew himself a blanket. The beavers still had their heads.

"I'm going to find myself a nice, plump blonde once I get that blanket made," he said. "Cuddle up for the winter." He eyed Grace, who waited in the car with her engine idling. "She'd do," he said. "She want to come inside?" I tried to laugh with him. I thought maybe he would ask me to stay, but he didn't. He joked he was eating better, without someone else to feed.

When there was nothing left of mine at home I made up excuses for Grace to drive me back: a diary that didn't exist, a favorite pillow. I found him curled up on the floor. Down the front of his shirt was a white, watery stain.

"There she is," he said, covering the stain with his hand. "Whoops."

He wrapped three fried pike in a napkin for me to share with Grace and Mandy. I thought of Grace eating around the eyes and tail fins and threw the fish into the brush, hiding the warm, oily napkin in my pocket.

Scotty Snotty brought lice back to school, and Mandy was the next person to get them, because he put his hat on her head during recess. We had to take baths together so Grace could shampoo our hair with medicine and set the timer for how long they took to die. After we were toweled off, but before the bathwater drained, we snuck back to look at the dead lice floating on top of the water. It was horrible but we had to see. The shampoo and combing left our hair shiny and soft, but then a week later she'd catch us scratching. Grace worked her way through all the shampoo brands. Eventually she said maybe it was me bringing them back each time I paid a visit to my dad.

I was homesick every day. But I didn't want to go back home, to the bathroom mirror covered in toothpaste splatter and the woods behind the house full of camouflaged traps and bleached bones, and the middle-of-the-night infomercials—the "Set It and Forget It" chicken rotisserie and the knife that cut through a can like it was butter.

I stole Nicorette from Dad's bedroom and let Mandy pop four pieces into her mouth, thinking she was chewing regular gum. It made her throw up.

Why do I do what I do? When I was little I'd wake up in the night and pee in the wicker wastebasket in the living room. I did this for months. The house was thick with the smell, and Dad blamed it on the dog. I knew he was thinking of getting rid of our dog, and I did it again, and he got rid of her. I really don't know why, I just did it because.

I began calling my dad at bedtime and begging him to come for me. When he finally came, Mandy and I could hear his truck's muffler from a mile away. The cats sprung from their chairs to hide under the bed. I met him in the dark drive with my garbage bag of clothes. Grace had kept my clothes neatly stacked in Mandy's dresser, smelling of ocean mist detergent.

I scrubbed the dishes piled high in Dad's sink, but rings still stained the coffee mugs, and the pot always held the black outline of rice grains where the rice had burned. When I called Mandy, Grace answered. "This is too hard," she said. "We love you, but you know it's been too hard." I hung up and went over to my cousin's and did whippits until my lips were numb.

All I can remember of the poem I slipped under Mandy's locker door is that it started "If there is a thing called love" and talked about her being like my sister. Mandy never wrote me back, but she wasn't mean about it.

Instead of school, I snaked the sink drain, wiped the black fur off the top of the ceiling-fan blades, cleaned the boathouse of old bait, and hosed down the cement where blood from field dressing deer had stained. I liked the sound of dirt sucking into the vacuum. I found pills stashed in a Folgers can beneath Dad's bed, and a rusted tackle box full of hooks, and with them another picture of Mom. She had her back to the camera, but I knew it was her from her long hair, as thick and wavy as a pelt. I tucked the picture into my pillowcase so I could feel its scalloped edge on my cheek.

It turned out Drill Kane was looking for a helper. My dad warned me about Drill—said as a teenager he stole lobsters from another man's trap, and when they'd fished together Drill hadn't tied the bait barrels down snug, and choppy waves sent them sliding overboard. He had my dad's type of weather-worn face but was fifteen years younger, with blond curls that got him picked on.

At the wharf Drill looked me over, circling, squeezing my biceps. He was shorter than me but he strutted like a bantam. The numbers *207* were tattooed across his throat, and I touched the area code with my fingertips. "That hurt?" I asked, but he just swallowed against my fingers. Drill dressed me in his old oil gear and it fit fine, but his boots and gloves made me look six years old.

"You'll do," Drill said. He bought me a new pair of boots that were still too big, so if I got caught on a trap it would drag the boot underwater instead of me. She was a beauty, Drill bragged, twenty-eight feet long, fiberglass, a John Deere engine he put in himself. Her name was the *Theresa*, after Drill's scabby-faced ex-girlfriend, but these days she's called the *Kimberly Rose*.

Being home with Kimmy now, I miss mornings alone on the bow most of all, when the wind wasn't stirred up yet, and light was just coming soft over the islands. I miss feeling the flex of new muscles that I didn't know I had, and the ache in my arms from hauling traps, and in my legs from bracing for balance on the slick deck. It felt good to be starved by the time we were done setting traps, feeling quick and light, and after that first day the boat's smell didn't bother me at all. It was with me all night, no matter how clean I got. Salt. In my dreams I'd bait traps and drop traps and empty traps and stack them.

We couldn't talk over the sound of the engine, or when we did we yelled ourselves hoarse. In Alma Harbor I pointed to the trees that hid Grace and Mandy's house and shouted,

"I lived there," and Drill shouted, "Only summer people live there." It felt like trespassing, checking traps in their harbor, but I was unrecognizable in Drill's gear.

I remember a lobster with no claws, wriggling like a snake beneath the others in the trap. Drill called it a pistol, said it shot its arms off to get free or because it got scared. He passed it to me, but I spooked when I held it, flung it overboard.

A lobsterman drowned, and for his funeral we joined a chain of boats that circled the harbor, our bow crashing up and down against the wake of the boat speeding in front of us. The *Theresa* was small against the others. Drill pushed her to the highest gear, the engine clunking and huffing blue exhaust. When we docked, it was so strange to be still again. My stomach pitched. I staggered up the dock ramp and puked. Drill said, "Little wimp," and we got in his truck and he pulled my head down into his lap and patted my hair until the feeling passed, his hand rough and noisy and warm against my ear.

One day out deep the engine quit. We drifted, and Drill refused to radio for help and burned his hand tinkering with the motor. Streaked with grease and swearing, he stripped his oil gear and jumped in. I jumped in too. He swam out too far for me to join him, and I waited for him in the water, a pure, cold pain that I couldn't get used to. When he swam back I wrapped my arms around his neck. "Doesn't it feel like I don't weigh a thing?" I said, and he said, "Feels like I'm holding nothing at all," and we bobbed together, numb, breathing.

That was the difference between them: Drill looked at me like he'd known me forever, and Dad looked at me like I was a stranger sneaking through the room.

Back then I didn't think too much about the times Dad touched me, except in a magical way, in which I thought the reason why my body grew so curvy so early was because of his hands. Everyone could see, like he'd watered me and I was a plant that grew overnight. But I didn't hate him.

The tree stump didn't kill my dad right away, just tossed him through the windshield and left him bleeding inside. He crashed on the shortcut road out of Treelaw, and no one passed by for too long, and his lung collapsed. The hospital called me in the middle of the night. I put my hand on his chest. He had tubes in his nose and his lips were dry and he kept licking them. I held my hand over his heart. I didn't hate him.

Winter was a tarped boat and the windows dark by three thirty. I let Drill's home absorb me into its own private smells and shadows and comfort. I painted buoys and mended traps and knit pockets for bait out of twine. Winter turned the skin at the nape of Drill's neck pink and raw. He shaved his blond curls. "You be the pretty one," he said. His scalp was covered in old scars that shined when the light hit them.

In our fridge there was just clam bellies and a jug of skim milk for Coffee Brandy. I bought a bag of oatmeal heavy as a baby so I could make hot breakfast and found brown specks crawling in it and picked them out for one bowl's worth, swallowing without looking at my spoon. I stayed in bed for days, fingering cigarette burns in the sheets, my muscles turning soft. My period skipped, and then it skipped again. Sometimes I lifted Drill's pet snake from its cage and it coiled on his pillow like black rope. Instead of sleeping I watched its slow blinking.

Our showerhead broke, and because of the water hitting the stall at the wrong angle paint chipped into the tub, and black mold bloomed across the tile. I went naked into the living room and straddled Drill. Around us the house was a shit storm: the garbage bag we'd been using as a shower curtain since Drill yanked the old one down, and our yard just a rutted ice pit, and in the freezer the frozen buckets of clam bellies, and the pigs eating the rotted ones, and the smell, musky and dark and low tide, that seemed to come from us. All of this was thick and terrible and Drill raking into me, the condom gone dry, I was sick. I was just sick.

When I called Grace the next month it was like she'd never stopped liking me. She wouldn't loan me money, but she hired me to clean house. She said that, with Mandy no longer living at home, she could use my company.

All of Grace's glasses were in the sink, rinsed and neatly stacked but dirty. She'd been drinking Ensure, she told me, because with just one person around there was no reason to cook, but she always made a point to pour it into a glass. This made it like a meal. Cleaning her house was like cleaning any other—the drain hair, the yellow stain ringing her toilet bowl, cat fur hidden behind the books on her shelves. The elephant and lion and bear figurines were stuck to the sill like no one had touched them since me. Grace's mildewed diaries were filled with the meals she and Mandy ate, the trips they took, the weather. I scanned the pages for my name.

In the bathroom I locked the door and climbed into their tub with no water. When I lifted my shirt my stomach looked soft and small, but soon the baby would show for good and my body could tell everyone for me. I picked a paper towel tube out of the trash and tried to press one end to my stomach so I could sing through it to my baby. I felt like the baby had a brain, and could hear me all right, even if the tube didn't reach. When I got out of the tub and looked in the mirror there was a red ring around my mouth.

Mandy's room was the same, minus the lipstick and glitter on the mirror and the cutout pictures that had been all over the walls. You could still see the outlines of our glow-in-the-dark solar system, and I scrubbed the glue gone. I crushed the stuffed animals she'd left behind into boxes and lay down on the floor.

When I woke up, at first I thought I was home. It was dark and I was covered with a blanket. There was one glow star left up by mistake, and I ripped it off and put it in my pocket and snuck downstairs.

"It's late," Grace said, startled awake from her sleep in front of the television. "Why don't you stay the night in Mandy's room?"

"I'm sorry I slept through my time," I said. "I've got to get home."

She emptied her wallet. "A little extra," she said, "to tide you over." She was leaving the next day for a week to visit Mandy. "You're sure you won't stay tonight?" she said. "Final offer. It's nice hearing you move around up there."

I said Drill was probably fit to kill me as it was, and she gave me a look like I was running away all over again, like I didn't have a home of my own that was worth making mention of.

Drill was sleeping when I climbed into bed, but his body greeted me, pressed up close, got hard. When I had him awake I pulled his cold hands to my stomach and described each room in Grace's house. With a pen I drew a blueprint on the back of my hand. In the morning, ink was stamped like bruises on my cheek, on my thigh, on my neck.

We drove into Alma. I knew the roads. I dream about those roads.

Drill looked like a little boy, scabbed knuckles gripping the big wheel. We sped through the dark past the outlines of houses, all of those summer mansions, each one empty.

I knew my baby had eyes on the front of its face by now, and fingers with fingernails, and ears, and could suck its thumb even, and there was a layer of hair over its body to keep it warm, or I'm not sure why, and when it moved inside me, which it hadn't done yet, it would feel something like butterflies.

The door was unlocked like I knew it would be. Inside, the house was cool and quiet and blue with moonlight. There was a bottle of diazepam on Grace's bedside table, and I considered taking all the pills in the bottle and lying down under the cool sheets of her neatly made bed. I could hear Drill throwing open drawers, and I opened the top drawer of Grace's dresser, took out her sweater, and pulled it on. It smelled like the color white. I imagined my baby would smell that way.

I tracked the sound of Drill's hands as they moved through the house, unlatching the little brass boxes on top of the mantel, the dining room cabinets, the Chinese trunk. I came out of her bedroom and watched him pull silver forks from her dish rack.

"We don't need to take all that," I said.

"I'm only taking what a burglar would take," said Drill. He carried her laptop and her stereo to the car. He unplugged her glass lamp.

"Leave it," I said. "She loves that."

"I'll build that baby the fanciest nursery you've ever seen," he said. "Two of them." He dumped wilted lilies onto the floor and took the vase. "You going to help, or have you changed your mind?" His voice whined. I took Grace and Mandy's photographs out of their gold frames.

The animal figurines were heavier than I remembered. I wrapped them up in one of Grace's scarves and held my hand over my mouth. I was cold with sweat. I didn't take them all. Drill came over and put his arms around me.

He wore Grace's big wool coat, and his fingers wiggled inside the pocket and pulled out a silver pocket watch. He grinned, the tops of his teeth white with plaque, and I could see his gums where molars were missing from drinking Coke not milk in his baby bottle, and the scars shimmered on his head. He held me, and his mouth felt like a gouge.

I told him to go start the engine. There was one room in the house I had forgotten, and I opened the closet door and squeezed through the coats to the secret storage space beneath the stairs, where it was so dark I couldn't see my own hands. I crawled over trash bags of bedding, splitting the plastic to find my own smell. The stale air was over-sweet, like my hair when I don't wash it. Like my pillows.

I didn't feel the baby kicking, not a thing, and I didn't sense it inside me either. When I found the far wall I leaned against it, breathing, thinking about the bath and Grace washing my hair. How good it felt to have my hair washed. How nice it was, to go to bed warm like that.

I waited for Grace to call. To have me come clean the mess, even, or to accuse me. I waited for someone to track us down, while we drove the long, dark stretches of highway, visiting pawnshop after pawnshop. Alone in my bedroom I waited for the police at the door, but mostly I waited for her.

My belly grew, and Kimmy was born, and Kimmy learned to walk, and I was still waiting on something.

No matter what. I left Drill to steer the boat today, carried Kimmy to the bow. I didn't want to tell him I'd seen Mandy. I just wanted to watch the bow cut through the water. The boat is where she naps best, all that white noise and rumbling and wind. When she stirred in my arms, mouth breathing and whimpering, I dug the gold elephant out of my bag, which on most days is her favorite, and tucked it into her fist. Her cheeks were red, almost feverish. I'd have to check her temperature when we got home.

Safe as Houses

"Speak to children about the incident in language they can understand," said the counselor on last night's local news. Harold hasn't quite figured out what language to use with his daughter. She shaved her legs with his razor, which he knew because the dulled blade nicked his neck and the handle smelled of her strawberry shampoo. She had this floral backless dress that she wore last week as they combed the beach, its deep pockets swollen with stones. Glancing up from scanning for blue glass the moment had caught him: Jenny bending toward the shoreline, her hair pulled over one shoulder, and the pale arch of her back belonging to a strange woman.

But then she lassoed him with seaweed rope and tripped ahead, hooting and skinny legged, her tattered sneakers squeaking on the rocks. Those sneakers still looked too big for her, and she'd toss them off wherever she pleased, in the bathroom or under the dining room table. The sneakers smelled funky, even out of the dryer, like kids' sneakers do. She wore his fleeces to the supermarket still, without embarrassment, the extra length of sleeve bunched at her elbows. Later, he'd pull one on and find gum wrappers in the pockets and that soapy sweet smell she left behind, the same way the crown of her head smelled when she was a baby.

In the morning he drives the bends at fifteen, for the power walkers pumping five-pound weights and the kids weaving lazily on bikes, but the road is deserted. Three police cruisers block the entrance to the town dock. The flag flutters at half-mast. Over breakfast he told Jenny the outline: a strange man attacked a summer girl but she escaped. He knows this talk is not sufficient, but he is waiting for her questions.

"I'm scared," says Jenny, fiddling with her seatbelt.

Her face hides behind the loose, honey-colored tangle of her hair. She's still wearing her Barrel of Monkeys pajamas.

"Me, too," he says. "But don't be. You won't feel a thing through all that Novocain and laughing gas. Lucky duck."

"I don't want braces anymore."

"Sure you do," he says. "You'll be the belle of the ball."

Somewhere along this stretch of road, Adelaide was forced into the white van. He scans the street as though there should be a sign—the shadow of the van, the shadow of the girl, seared into the pavement.

* * *

Now he waits in the lobby while dental hygienists whisper from behind the receptionist's desk. "Poor girl," they say, and "in broad daylight," and "not here, never in a million years." Gestures stand for the details of the crime—heads shaken, hands held to their mouths.

"Dad," calls one of the hygienists, "she's asking for you." Jenny is reclined in the dental chair, her lips pulled back from her teeth with wads of cotton. There is little room for him. He sits in a chair in the corner. Jenny's hand appears from under her paper bib and she waves at him. He waves back.

"I'm going to give you some nitrous oxide now," says the dentist, whose hairy hand loops a tube over her ears and tucks it into her nostrils. "Tell me when you feel it."

"I don't feel anything," says Jenny.

Harold watches as her clenched hands relax.

"Maybe now. I feel something." Her words are full of tongue and spit. They've tucked an apparatus into her mouth to stretch it wider.

"I feel something," she says, a few minutes later. "I feel it."

"Doing good, dear," says the dental hygienist.

"OK there, just a little pressure," says the dentist. His big blue-gloved fingers strain against a pair of pliers. Jenny is breathing hard, and then there is blood on his gloves and on her bib. The tooth is small, with a long root. The dentist drops the tooth into a metal tin.

"Dad," Jenny says.

He can just make it out. There is no way to stop what is happening: the dentist readying his pliers, the hygienist with her sucking tool inside Jenny's mouth. The sucker changes pitch when it catches on the inside of her cheek. The dentist holds up a finger toward Harold when he tries to go to her.

"Please," says the dentist.

"Almost done," says the hygienist. "You're doing great."

"Dad," Jenny says, again. She is wild eyed, and her stretched mouth makes him think of a warhorse flipped onto its back.

"It's like I'm in a well." The word "well" is nearly lost. He has to strain to find it.

Another tooth plinks into the tin.

"Please keep quiet," says the dentist.

"Doing just fine," says the hygienist.

"Keep your tongue still," the dentist says, "quiet, that's it."

"Down in a well," Jenny gargles. "Looking at you."

"I'm right here, sugar."

He moves to the foot of her chair, and squeezes her sneaker.

"But you're way up there."

"I'm going to have to give her the midazolam," the dentist says, his voice soft with anger. "She'll be awake, but no fear at all with this stuff. Just a nice twilight sleep."

The hygienist is swabbing Jenny's arm, preparing an IV. "Just a tiny pinch," she says.

Jenny's eyes close and her feet splay.

"There she goes," says the dentist. "Good girl. Now if you don't mind waiting over there please."

Harold lets go of Jenny's sneaker, returns to his chair, sits on his hands. The room is quiet. He tries to clench his jaw against the click of his chattering teeth. "Air conditioning too chilly, hon?" the hygienist asks him. "Why don't you grab a cup of coffee in the waiting room. She won't notice."

He wants to stay but there's a twitching around his mouth.

"You sure?"

"Dead to the world."

His skin is pricking, electric. He tries not to rush through the lobby to the parking lot. Outside it's Jenny that surrounds him, some kind of sweet distillate. The feeling has been accelerating since last night, his daughter growing into detailed relief like a print left to etch too long in acid. The smell of her ChapStick as she kisses his cheek before bed, how she hums brushing her teeth, the puff of her almost snore through his bedroom wall.

The feeling withdraws. It is only gathering strength for the next wave. He goes back inside, through the lobby, into the operating room. The hygienist is cleaning the blood crusted at the corners of Jenny's mouth, which is still gaping, and the blood and the gaping mouth root themselves into his chest. He feels the way he expected to feel in the weeks Jenny's mother was dying. That all of it, even the most vulgar details, would come home to his heart. Before they were married, before Jenny, he was certain that he'd love her face in old age, that their job as lovers was to love each other's faces in all their forms. But the beginning wasn't too far before she got sick, which was the end. Her face grew old when she was still young, and her breath turned sour from too much sleep. Her head resting on his shoulder radiated heat, leaving a crescent of sweat behind on his sleeve. The details were not precious, but terrifying. The coated tongue, the mushroomy smell before he got her in the bath. Her nostrils were flared and animal as he held her hand at the end of it, Jenny wailing from her crib. Only after she died did grace shake loose, the twisted sheet stripped from her bed, the fresh one filling like a sail before settling smooth.

They prop Jenny up, and tears drain out of her ears. She's awake again, but she can't keep her eyes open. They tell him to keep the cotton wads in her cheeks, to stanch any bleeding. She shuffles against him, her face pressed to his shirt pocket. He carries her to the car, her long legs knocking against his knees. In the car she huffs and pulls the cotton from her mouth, pink spit stranding from her chin to her hand. He finds the soggy tuft inside her fist and tucks it back into her cheek.

"Dad," she says as Harold's tugging off her sneakers. She is propped up in bed, head lolling. Her hair hangs in her face. She blows it away. He can picture her as a woman, whiskey drunk in college.

"Hey, sugar."

"Questions," she says. "Can you answer them?" The cotton blurs her words.

"Sure."

"Socks off please," she says. Her toes move around inside her socks. He takes them off and pulls the blanket to her chin. He pats her hair, and her breathing slows.

"When's the dentist?"

"We're back from the dentist. It's all done."

"I'm worried," she says.

"What for? You were a champ."

"She was raped?"

"Yes," he says. He remembers to breathe.

"Who?" He fishes the wet wad from her mouth and throws it in the bedside wastebasket.

"A summer girl. Vacationing with her grandparents." Jenny has heard this much, last night. He told her after the phone tree people called. He did not use the word rape. She didn't ask any questions then.

"Adelaide," she says. "Right, right. Oh no." She puts a hand over her eyes. "But she's so beautiful. She was always waving to me. Every time I saw her, she smiled and waved."

Adelaide walked every morning, fast, but never with mail or a dog giving her a reason to walk. She wore white Keds. Her mother was from Jamaica, her father from Connecticut. She had blue beads on the ends of her braids. Everyone in town waved to everyone else, but Adelaide would wave and smile at him like he'd just walked through the door after being away for too long. Like his was the face she'd been hoping to see.

"Oh no," Jenny is saying, shaking her head back and forth. "She was so happy." Harold closes his eyes. It is terribly easy to watch the film reel continue: The van slowing beside her as she turned to smile. How her face must have changed as the man drew a gun and pointed it to her temple. How it must have changed again when he pulled a hood over her head. Fear, with no one to see it.

Jenny's quiet for a minute with her eyes closed, but they're twitching behind her lids.

"Wait," she says. "How'd he get her?"

"He had a gun," he says.

"Where'd he take her?"

"Back behind the cemetery."

"So close," she says.

While Adelaide was being attacked, Harold was weeding the garden. The man must have taped her mouth. Harold surely would have heard her if she'd screamed.

"She got away?"

"Yes, sweetie, she got away. Afterward she ran. She was lucky." Jenny's eyes stay shut. He kisses her cheek goodnight. Her skin is hot, tight with a slight swelling.

"He got away too?" she says.

"The police say there's no way he'd stick around. Probably escaped out of state. Maybe he got out by boat, but they'll get him. The coast guard searched the harbor. He's not coming back here."

She's still and silent under her blanket. He listens to her breathing slow. "He's back," she says, her words softened, dream-speak.

* * *

42

The wad of dollars warms in her fist as she walks up the driveway. She hates the sailing lessons, how the instructors make her wear a mildewed orange life jacket, stiff from spending winter in a basement. She hates how the older boys capsize the dinghies on purpose, then swim quickly to the dock to watch as she doggy paddles in, salt water lapping at her mouth. But sailing is an excuse to get her away from the chicken soup and lime Jell-O, crossword puzzles, cartoon marathons, Dad's anxious face. She had to beg him to let her walk the five minutes to the dock alone. She hasn't been outside in days, and her legs feel wobbly. She is walking away from sailing and chaperones, along the dirt road that leads to the graveyard. She must have intended to lie to her dad all along, but she discovers the lie as she watches her feet in their course toward the place she is no longer allowed to go.

The leaves on the oak trees leading to the graveyard are mottled with hot pink fungus. Pepperbush, which her dad points out every summer and Jenny has never noticed before, is in full bloom and the air is spicy and over-sweet. Hidden in the leaves as she turns down the graveyard drive is a scrap of weathered blue fabric. She imagines it is part of a girl's dress, but it's only a fake flower. She tucks the dirty silk petals behind her ear and walks up to the graves, putting a hand on her mother's warm stone.

The headstones in the new graveyard are shiny and clean, etched with soaring eagles and lobster boats trailing wakes into the rising sun. She weaves through them. Behind the new graveyard, the headstones in the old graveyard are black with age. Lichen grows over the engravings. Many of them are nameless children's graves, no bigger than schoolbooks.

She is afraid, but she has always been afraid. In the parking lot of Home Depot, listening to *Prairie Home Companion* with the doors locked, waiting for her dad to pick up some lumber, she is afraid. She's afraid when she gets home from school, as she eats her pudding cup and watches TV alone before he gets home, and she is afraid when she isn't alone also, falling asleep to the quiet hum of the house. Sometimes her fear takes the form of an imagined man in a black mask, and it isn't so much what he could do to her that scares her, but that when he did it she'd be alone. That afterward she would never be let back into her life the way it was before. And now this fear is real and in the world, escaping by back roads in his white van.

When she slaps at her neck, her hand comes back dotted with blood. The mosquitoes make a veil around her hair, drawn by her shampoo. There is no sign that anything terrible happened here. The graveyard and the main road curve out of view. The ground grows soft; tire ruts cup muddy water. There is a stink in the air, fetid but sweet. The leaves on the trees are flipped, their pale undersides puffed to the sky. Rain is on its way.

She rounds the corner to find the forest flooded by a yellow swamp. Row after row of trees grow out of the water, skinned of their bark, brittle and sun bleached, riddled with woodpecker holes. A ring of scum encircles each trunk. Jenny always imagined the woods at her town's center as lush and dark, pines too crowded to run through, but here it is, ruined by beavers. She remembers overwatering the garden lettuce, how the roots of the dying plants rose from the soil like slow spiders. The pines submerged at the lake's edge have boughs tipped with light green new growth, but she knows they are done for.

She untangles the blue flower from her hair, turning from the water, fighting the urge to run. The bog gapes at her back. She watches her thighs pressing uphill, and counts her breath in tens until the main road comes into view. The humidity raises a musky smell from her shirt. Safe in the new graveyard, she puts the blue flower and the sailing money on her mom's headstone.

"Please," she says. It is an offering that stands for a prayer, for Adelaide, and seeping into that a second prayer, for herself. "Thank you."

That night she scuffs her sneakers on the pavement, listening to Freddy while pretending she's not listening. Her dad has allowed her to go on the Community Night scavenger hunt, because they walk around in a group, she argued, plus there are chaperones.

"Wasn't supposed to hear it, because they were in the front with the radio and thought I was sleeping, but I heard," Freddy says.

"Come on, man," says Jake. "Just spill." He plucks a half-smoked cigarette from the library lawn and fumbles to light it. His lips are chapped. Jake's one of the terrible boys from sailing who threw her off the dock last summer. He exhales a weak curl of smoke. He's probably sixteen, a chaperone, but he's short and as small as Jenny, his braces gluey with rubber bands.

He claps his hands. "All right, little ones. Let's get this show on the road." They're headed to Freddy's house for a marble, the first item on the scavenger-hunt list. Jenny tries to tuck herself into the group of chaperones. The littler kids run ahead, squealing.

Jake hands the half-smoked cigarette to Freddy. "Sick," Freddy says, but he puffs anyway. "Gag. Wet."

"So what did you hear?" asks Liz. Jenny walks in step beside her.

"I don't know," says Freddy. "It's really bad."

"Whatever," Liz says.

"Mixed company, I mean," he says, his voice low. Liz looks at Jenny.

"I just mean, how old are you?" Freddy asks.

"Nah, man, she's cool," says Jake. He throws his arm over Freddy's shoulder.

Jenny nods. "I'm old enough," she says, so quiet she's not sure if they hear.

Freddy drops his voice. "They said this girl, Adelaide, was douched by this guy, after he, you know." He laughs like the air is being pressed out of him.

"What a douche bag," Jake says. Freddy punches his arm, and Jake lurches into Jenny.

"Sorry, too soon," he says, stumbling. He steadies himself, looping his arm around Jenny's waist, slowing the two of them down. "I missed you in sailing today."

"I hate sailing," she says. "Thanks to you."

"Wow," he says. "Big talk. Feisty." His hand teases the belt loop on her jeans. Linked like this, they are clumsy. They can't keep up.

"You scared?" he asks.

"No."

"You didn't ask what of."

"What, then?"

"You know," he says. The laces of his sneaker have come undone. They flick at her ankle.

"Maybe they'll catch him," she says.

"Doubt it. Not without the DNA. The douche, right? You get that?"

"Sure," she says.

"So how old are you now?"

"Thirteen in August."

"OK," he says, slow, nodding.

"You?"

"Too old for you." His hand is under her shirt now, on the curve of her hip. "I'm just kidding," he says. "You should have seen your face. You're dangerous."

The rest of the group is far ahead. Freddy turns and whistles back at them as he rounds the bend in the road, out of sight.

"You don't need to be scared," he says.

"I'm not."

"Sure you are." He puts a hand on her head, stopping her. "But he doesn't want you. You're white. So don't worry about it."

She watches the moon's reflection tracking across the water behind him. She watches the slow blink of a satellite move through the sky.

"I want your picture," he says, pulling her to face him. He rocks her in the road, a slow dance. "What are you thinking about?"

"Why?"

"Because I want to know."

"Why do you want my picture, I mean."

"To show my friends back home how hot you are."

She smiles at her sneakers.

"Who made you so sweet?" he asks. He pushes her bangs back from her forehead.

"I don't know," she says.

"Come on."

"My parents, maybe."

He throws his head back to laugh. "That's good," he says. "That's really good."

"Shouldn't we catch up?" she asks. She wipes her palms on her shorts.

"Don't worry," says Jake. "I'll walk you home."

He licks his lips each time he leans in to kiss her. His kisses taste like smoke and sesame seeds. He leads her down to the beach. She's thought about this kind of thing, but now that it's happening all she can think is how relieved she will feel to be back in her bedroom, in her pajamas, under her quilt. The rocks on the beach are still warm. A loon wails across the water. Jake gets his hand under the cup of her bra, and then his mouth. When he fumbles with his buckle and pulls his pants to his ankles she sits up and straightens her shirt. He pulls her hand over to the hole in his boxers.

"This OK?" he breathes. She shakes her head.

"No? You want to stop?" Her hand is in his hand, she has let him lead her, and now she is touching him. It is a curiosity to feel it, small and soft, this thing she has never seen up close. They are touching him together. At first her hand is loose in his, but when her fingers start to understand what he wants they can't help but move in the right way. He grows inside her palm. When his hand darts into her shorts and under the elastic of her underwear, she is mostly embarrassed that he is feeling the thatch of hair.

"Wanna kiss my neck?" he asks. "Like that." Jake's skin is salty. His belt buckle jabs into her leg. His fingers begin to move against her. She is dry and closed to him, and then she is full of his fingers, their pressure and their ache. She lies still but then, as with her hand, her body moves on its own without her, hips back and forth, rocking against his hand. Her breath knocks out of her and into his ear.

She can feel her pulse in the sockets where they pulled out her teeth.

* * *

Harold wakes to Jenny in his bedroom doorway.

"Dad," she says, the hallway light on behind her, the web of her hair illuminated. He can't see her face. "There's someone at my window."

He is too slow rising to the surface, getting out of bed, fumbling with the lamp.

"I'm scared," she whispers. She is crying. "Someone's there."

His grandfather's shotgun is hidden in the back of the closet, an unloaded heirloom, its bullets secreted in a leather pouch inside a shoebox. He does not know if it will fire.

"Stay here," he says, walking down the hallway to her bedroom, heart snapping. "It's probably nothing." But as he says this he hears scrambling in the branches of the apple tree that grazes Jenny's open window, and there it is, a figure shifting in the outside darkness, a black outline against the black branches. He moves slowly toward the window, waiting, not breathing, watching as the dark shape develops into a fat raccoon.

"Get out of here," he shouts, pounding the window until the glass cracks. The tree squirms with life. Behind the one raccoon, he realizes, are a dozen more, unafraid, slinking from the branches to snatch fallen fruit on the kitchen roof, climbing the drainpipe paw over paw, some of them hanging upside down. He watches them clean the tree of apples, its shaken limbs dropping ripe fruit.

"Dad?" Jenny calls from the hallway. Eyes glint in the tree's leaves. "Is it safe?"

He can hear the soft wet sound of the raccoons chewing, but beyond that there is something else. He holds his breath, listening. A noise in the night: deliberate and human and close. Like the blade of an ax hacking into a tree. When he reaches out to close the window a branch grazes his hand and he recoils involuntarily, shuddering with revulsion. Sound carries easily across the bay. *The noise must be a boat,* he thinks, *waves knocking its hull, or some clanging loose part.*

After he tucks Jenny back in bed he steps outside for some air. He hasn't locked the house since he bought it, thirty years earlier, because no one in the town locks anything. But now he locks the door on his daughter even though the threat is, in all likelihood, long gone.

The strange noise has disappeared, replaced by the shrill din of crickets crawling in their field. His eyes won't adjust to the dark circle of surrounding pines. Close, very close now, a sound presents itself. A body brushing boughs. Twigs cracking, then silence. Like footsteps circling.

"Hello?" he says. He hears, in the word, how his spit has gone tacky. He feels absurd. Frightened, probably, by another raccoon. He doesn't move. He watches. The motion sensor light on the porch flickers on and off. There is no denying a rustling in the leaves. Dew from the grass climbs up the legs of his pajamas. The moon slips out from the clouds. He imagines how he would look to someone watching from the woods—a gray-haired father in reading glasses, pajamas, and slippers, but he feels animal. If someone came at him he could tear them apart. Ten minutes go by. Twenty. The woods are full of night noise, crawling and skittering, just that, and the wind blowing through the tops of the pines.

Jenny wakes to "Wild Horses." When she was little they would slow dance to this song, her feet on her dad's feet, and when she got older they would still dance a little, in their own private way, to wake her up before school. She knows the deal is that she'll come downstairs before the song is over, but she stays in bed until the last chorus. He is waiting at the bottom of the stairs, and when he sees her he starts to dance, like he hasn't been waiting.

"Hey, kiddo," he says. "Nice monkey PJs." By now the song has ended. He hunches over the CD player, searching for repeat.

The kitchen floor is cold on her bare feet. He kicks his slippers over to her. They are warm from him.

"Good scavenging last night?"

"I guess," she says.

"Did those summer kids behave themselves? Was everyone cool?"

She sighs. "Same as always."

"You got it, my teen. No more questions."

She can't make eye contact, but then she does, and he looks back, and the moment moves forward. He is whistling, full of kitchen bustling, flipping pancakes. Sleeplessness tingles in her stomach, clenching it. Her scrambled eggs are wet.

Upstairs she locks the bathroom door and folds her pajamas neatly on the counter. Her nipples are embarrassing. The blonde hair circling her belly button is embarrassing. Her face in the mirror is slack and strange. She climbs into the shower. The earthy sharpness of Jake's deodorant and sweat is all over her, rising off her shoulders with the shower's steam. She unhooks the showerhead and holds its weight in her hands, testing the pressure, turning the faucets until the water runs cool. She presses the showerhead gently between her legs. At first the feeling is nice. She pushes the lip of the metal inside her. A fullness snakes through her body, the water a spreading coolness. She thinks of the graveyard, of Adelaide in a dusty blue dress, the color of the fake flower. The same cool stream of water inside them both, cleaning them out. Her body turns the water warm and it drains down her leg. She feels better already.

Drawing Blood

I have a recurring nightmare—I am standing in the street outside my home, as it looked in 1918. A figure emerges from the darkness at the far end of the street, but something isn't right, and as they come closer I realize it is you. You stagger, as though drunk. Sometimes when I have my eyes closed and nothing at all on my mind, in the midst of all that darkness you emerge in your white nightgown, trailing a fur coat behind you in the dust, stumbling closer until I can see your face, eyes half-closed, mouth slack and glistening.

Nicholas has been dead twenty years, you'll be glad to know, and like I said he stopped seeing me in a womanly kind of way more than twenty before that.

I didn't maintain my figure. Mother wore her boned corset into her fifties, long after they went out of fashion, and a girdle in her eighties, even though my father was long dead. Even near the end, when she couldn't remember our names, each morning she'd remember to put on her girdle. She flirted with her grandsons when they came to visit her, whom she called by my father's name, and groped when they were alone. They slapped away her hands, but she persisted. She was stubborn.

All growing up I watched your house from my upstairs window. I can remember when I was five years old—this is the age my memories begin—waking up in the night to howling in the street. It was your father, doubled over, from laughter or tears it wasn't clear, and he was making strange noises, babble strung together with song. In my memory he was perfectly dressed in a dark wool suit, still wearing his hat, which he held to his head while he bent over to vomit. I don't know how long I watched him performing for the darkened houses on our street before your mother brought him inside.

That scene played out so many times that eventually your mother stopped ushering him in at night. He made noise until he exhausted himself, sometimes singing or talking, more often, as time passed, crying, and eventually he'd lie down on the porch, or on bad nights, when he couldn't climb the front steps, he'd curl up in the garden. Sometimes when I woke at dawn I'd go to the window and he'd still be outside sleeping, but always by the time I made my way to the schoolhouse he was gone. Over the years I stopped going to the window when I heard his wailing, for even something as terrible and alluring as a man losing his dignity became less interesting in time. Instead of watching, with my toes and fingers pricked by cold, my face pressed to the frozen glass, I stayed under the warmth of my down comforter.

I never saw you or your mother moving around inside your house. It was as though the two of you and the house itself, with its sloping roofline and peeling planks and the yellowed, overgrown lawn, were all part of the set for the show that was your father.

I saw your father asleep in the garden on the day he died, and I'll never know if he was dead by the time I saw him or if he died shortly thereafter, if perhaps there was a chance I could have saved him. Instead I pretended the dark of his coat was a rock or mound of earth. It was cold that day, or must have been, because although I remember walking swiftly past your house and off to school, sweating under my wool coat and scarf, by the time your mother found him he had frozen to death.

Before that no one really looked at you—gangly and ordinary, twelve years old like me but a head taller. Homeschooled. You used to go to church, until one Sunday your father threw up in the middle of the sermon, right into his hand, then knelt down as if he were praying and wiped it on the kneeler. After that you didn't go anymore. You always wore simple white dresses, and your mother ironed your pleats and polished your boots. She did the same for herself, and kept the hair on both your heads braided in a tight coil, so that before your father died people felt only small, manageable amounts of pity when they looked at you two. But after he froze the pitiable details emerged, as though you were a picture just then developing. Your boots, with the frayed laces and uneven soles, and your dresses—when one looked closely it was clear the hem had been let out and let out again, though your skirt still didn't cover your ankles. The felt on your winter coat was threadbare at the shoulder, and after your father's memorial service I noticed your mother walking with her arm around your shoulder and her hand covering the threadbare spot, whether on purpose or not I wasn't sure but she stayed like that, stitched awkwardly to your side, even as she accepted handshakes and embraces.

It was unsettling to watch my mother in the throes of her pity. After your father's memorial service she lingered longer by you and your mother's side than anyone else, her eyes brimming with a strange and eager softness. It was a look I'd never seen her wear before. And when the bank foreclosed on your house with the intention of demolishing it and selling the land, my mother knocked on your door and implored that we were in need of a servant and our guest room was just sitting empty, which wasn't true—it was full of many of my books, dolls, clothes, and paintings. Your mother accepted the offer on your behalf, though she would move into the city and stay with her sister. I spent days tromping up and down the attic stairs in preparation for your arrival.

When you first moved in I didn't like your sudden presence in our home. I didn't like hearing the sound of you singing in the room next to mine, or seeing your drawers and stockings displayed on the laundry line with my family's finer things. We were cozily settled before you arrived. Weekends when we were all home together my brother Ben would sit in the grass sketching birds and my father would fall asleep with the newspaper and I'd sing while Mother played the parlor piano. For dinner there was a roast, for dessert a plum pudding, and on occasions that my father had a good week at the office, Mother made her rum-soaked apple upside-down cake. I liked the predictability of my family's orbits and habits, and I knew what occupied them, as though we were forever rehearsing a staged production.

You upset this, always lurking in the corner while we finished our plates of cake, waiting for my mother and me to stop singing at the piano so you could dust the piano top. You were constantly watching. Your watching turned us from a family into a performance of one.

Every time I caught myself laughing freely, the next moment there you'd be, clearing our plates, and a newly familiar feeling of shame would wash over me. It was as if you wore the shame of your father's death as perfume, the scent lingering in our rooms even after you finished the day's cleaning and retired.

The years passed this way and we exchanged only the sparest remarks. I remember one day we were alone in the house together and I wanted something to eat but you were in the kitchen preparing dinner. I waited until my stomach was wound with hunger but you would not leave, and when I finally resolved to enter the kitchen I gathered our cat into my arms to use as a kind of shield. You were punching a lump of dough on the countertop and singing to yourself. I crept silently behind you. When you turned and saw me you yelped and the cat scrambled around in my arms, drawing blood.

You put down the piece of dough you were molding and held my arm just as carefully. There was a long line of beaded blood across my wrist, and you dabbed at it with the corner of your apron until I pulled away and said not to bother ruining it. At the next dinner I kept glancing at the three dark spots staining the corner of your apron, and for many dinners after that, as the blood would not wash clean.

Four years passed where I didn't know you but came to know the sounds of you in the room next to mine—the creaking of the floorboards at dawn and the bath you took each evening, the swish of your hand testing the temperature of the water and then later the swish of your long hair whipping back and forth as you rinsed it clean. I could hear you singing and, before bed, if I held my breath, I could hear you whispering what must have been prayers.

Not to mention how beautiful you became over those years would be like lying. I permitted myself to watch you only as a shape in my peripheral vision.

For three weeks I had chill fever, and for three weeks you entered my room and pressed a cool cloth to my forehead and the back of my neck, or dabbed it in water and held it to my cracked lips. The blurred edges of my thoughts seemed to crystallize when you touched me.

It was a Saturday. Mother played the piano and my father read his newspaper, but my brother was fighting in the war instead of watching for birds. Mother continued to play the same lively tunes that she'd always played, her feet pumping the pedals. I was practicing the foxtrot for the upcoming winter dance, and as you came in carrying a tray of tea cookies my mother halted her playing.

"Why don't you practice with Eva?" she said. "Suppose someone asks her to the dance, well then you both can learn."

"I couldn't," you said, and shook your head, but my mother had already risen from the piano bench and was pushing you toward me saying, "Go on, go on, have a little fun for once, for God's sake."

You shook your head, smiling, and the gap between your teeth flashed at me, secret as a wink. I took your hands. Right away mine felt overly warm against your cool, dry palms.

"Come on now," my mother said, "not like you're two corpses," and she grabbed your arms and shook them, "loose, loose, like that, good," and then she clutched you close and spun you around. "There," she said, moving me back into place. "I won't have a daughter of mine not knowing how to properly woo a beau—Eva, you be the man, that's right, and pull her tight. That will do. Ready?"

We circled and circled the room, stepping on each other's feet and laughing, while Mother played through her entire ragtime repertoire, and then she switched to a waltz. I had never heard you laugh. You snorted. "Don't be imbeciles, go on now, dance it nicely," Mother said. We held on tightly to each other. With your height it was like dancing with a man, and my chin tucked into the long white of your neck as our circles slowed. I was breathing hard from our earlier dancing and my breath warmed against your skin and stirred up the smell of your hair and pressed close like this I could feel how your body fit with mine. My skin burned beneath the layers of my white cotton dress.

"Good work," Mother said, halting the waltz. Her voice made me flinch. "Time for lunch, what have you cooked up, Eva?" Could she see the way I leaned into you? How my leg fit between yours, keeping the beat? Through lunch I felt as I hoped I would if God chose to reveal his presence to me—a golden tightening behind my sternum that spread throughout my body, warming me like liquor, lighting me from the inside. My father didn't look up from his paper as we ate but nodded occasionally at my mother, who talked and talked. Your smell—now I'd learned it and when you leaned over me to clear my plate away it lifted me like the first earthy days of spring.

In my dream I realize you have poisoned yourself. I realize because as you get closer there is white froth at your mouth.

From my bedroom window, I can see where your old house used to stand. Now it is a deli and liquor store, where men gather to smoke and hoot.

Were I to find you, and talk to you, what would you remember? Your father, your house, our afternoon of waltzing? Do you remember that before my mother said "good work" and stopped our dancing I had my lips parted against your neck?

You were never my friend. We never walked together in the street with armfuls of books, red cheeked, laughing over boys. I could barely look at you in others' company, after you snuck into my bedroom, quiet as moonlight, on the night we received word of my brother's death.

I could not stop my crying. I was so afraid that when I said, "I'm all right," it was as if I traveled outside my body to watch myself speak. I pulled back the cover and you climbed in beside me. We curled knee to knee. Nothing touched but our kneecaps. I watched the candlelight on your face and you watched me crying and we fell asleep like that, listening to the soft sound of my mother crying in her bedroom down the hall. In the morning you were gone, but you snuck back the next night, and the next, coming closer to me in the bed each time until our warmth made me toss off the blankets, and then your tongue was in my mouth, and what could I do but learn how to dance with it, and when I did the kiss was slower. I felt like I hadn't been warm since winter started; not layered with Mother's wool sweaters that ringed my neck with rash, not helping you peel the boiled potatoes, their steam darting around my fingers, but as we moved together I was warm as I'd ever been, slippery against you.

Before my mother died she saw things everywhere: my brother as a little boy crawling across her bedspread, my father in the face of the nurse who bent to tuck her breathing tube back into her nose, and once she looked around the hospital room, awestruck, and stroked her arm as though it were a baby saying "Mary, Mary, Mary," and when I said, "I'm right here, Mom," she looked at me as if I'd slapped her.

Another day she opened her eyes wide and said in wonderment, "The woman is trying to save the crane. Its wing is broken, see that? Would you look at the size of that bird." She leaned forward in the bed, pointing. "What a marvel. Oh! What's happening now?"

I said, "There's nothing there."

I regret that.

She said, "Is that so? How funny this is," lay back and didn't say another word and by the next afternoon she was dead.

It was a Saturday when Nicholas Laramie came to offer his respects for the death of my brother, which turned into him and my father dipping into the good scotch before lunchtime and by three they'd played through all of Ben's favorite songs on the piano, red faced, swaying on the bench, refusing lunch and my mother's entreaties that they not make so much noise, pounding their fists on the piano if I didn't clap from where I sat reading in the corner. At four my father excused himself to go upstairs and nap, but when I went upstairs after him I heard the sound of his retching behind the bathroom door.

I snuck back down the stairs and it was just Nicholas alone in the parlor, his head resting on the piano keys. He staggered from the bench and plopped beside me on the love seat where I'd returned to read my book. "Mary," he said. "Please. I'd like to take you to the dance."

"You're not well," I said. "I'm not going. Not so soon after Ben." He reached over and snapped my book closed.

"Why do you have to break my heart," he said, wiping his leaky eyes on the back of his wrist.

From far away Nicholas gave the illusion of being handsome, with his blond hair greased back and a straight-toothed smile. My mother had always said he was the handsomest of Ben's friends, that were she my age she'd be smitten with him, but up close I saw what she didn't—how pomade glistened at his temples, the strange patches of dry skin at the corners of his mouth.

"Oh come on," I said, "you're like a brother to me." My throat hurt from the effort of not crying. Ben hadn't even known Nicholas all that well. I thought of my sick father, a man who never drank, not even on communion.

"I want to go with you because you're the only girl I know who'll let me talk close to her," he said, slipping his hand onto my knee and letting it warm there. We both watched it.

"What do you say, sweet Mary May?" And then you walked in with the tea and didn't look at me and started setting the table. He kept his hand on my leg.

I said, "Why don't you ask Eva, if you want to go to the dance so badly."

The teacups rattled on your serving tray. "I don't know how to dance," you said.

"Look at those lovely arms. You were born for dancing." He took the tea tray from your hands.

"I'll play," he said to me, "and we'll teach her a thing or two."

"Please, let's not," you said under your breath. He started in on the piano, the notes galumphing along in unrelenting cheer.

I didn't notice Mother, in her bathrobe at the top of the stairs, until she shouted down, "For the love of God quit that racket." She braced herself on the railing as though she might fall.

"Deepest apologies, ma'am," said Nicholas, "just trying to make Eva dance. I've got it in my mind to take her, if you can spare a night."

The bathroom door opened and my father lurched out, ashen as I'd ever seen him. He slumped down on the step beside my mother and said, "You keep on playing, son."

"Jim," said Mother, "can't you grant me one moment of peace?"

He flicked his hand at her. "Keep on, I said."

"Sir?" said Nicholas. My father hung his head in his hands and bellowed, "This is my house, and I'm asking you to play." Nicholas started in on "A Bird in a Gilded Cage" and halfway through my father looked up, searched the room for me, and said, "You sing, Mary. You used to be a canary. Why don't you sing anymore?" and so I forced my mouth to sing the last verse and you and everyone watched me, because it was better than watching my father, who had begun to cry.

When you came to my room that night I was angry as I kissed you. Our teeth kept clicking together.

Still, on the day of the dance I insisted you wear my silk underthings, my finest necklace, my tortoiseshell comb in your hair, and I draped my velvet jacket over your shoulders.

"I don't want to go," you said.

I said, "Don't worry. Nicholas picked you. You're one of us now."

I didn't tell you that you looked beautiful. Instead I made a catalog of all the ways in which you weren't—how on most days your hair hung in two braids and at night you worked the tangles out from behind your ears, or the subtle lisp you had when you spoke, too much spit in your mouth. How your eyelids grew shiny with oil by the end of the day. The fine, dark hair that trailed in a line from your belly button. The dimples on the backs of your thighs.

When Nicholas arrived he leaned into me and said, "Don't worry, I'll have her back early." He used breath spray, and I could smell what the mint masked, a warm, milky, babyish smell. The two of you walked away arm in arm, leaving me on the porch peeling potatoes. It was cold and gray outside, and my hands were freezing, but I couldn't stay in the house another minute. I could hear when the band started up and behind the dance hall, in the far field, the cows lowing. I thought of you, spinning and spinning, the heat of dancing stirring up the smell of your skin and Nicholas's hands on your back. And I hated it, I hated you, and I looked down at the knife I was using to peel the potatoes and cut a deep line across my palm, surprised at the initial lack of blood.

I walked toward the dance hall, my hand wrapped up in my skirts. It started to sleet. Wetness climbed up my hem, my soaked skirt lashing my ankles. There was a big circle of light surrounding the dance hall where kids were chatting and laughing, but I stood far enough away in the darkness of the street that I couldn't see who they were or their outfits. From inside the hall the music picked up, and with it hooting and laughter. I listened for you. My cut throbbed.

After the dance, you came to my room to return my things. Normally you were so carefully quiet when you came to me, but this time you were louder than you should have been. You unclasped your shoes in the doorway and kicked them off. Your frizzy hair was haloed, backlit by the hallway light. You crawled into my bed, in your wet coat, in your party dress, and unpinned your hair. Loosed and dark, it snaked over my pillow, smelling of cigarette smoke. Your breath was sour and close.

I noted a small cut, like a beauty mark on your upper lip.

When I woke up again you were gone and my jade necklace was on the pillow beside me. I lay in bed fingering its beads, still warm from your body, and in my head started to pray the rosary, though I didn't want to. A habit of the hands.

On the nights that followed I said nothing about the bruises on your arms and legs, one in your armpit, one in the curve of your neck that you hid with a high collar.

You returned my silk underthings clean and faintly stained. I didn't think about it. I told myself it was your time of the month to bleed, though I knew when you bled. We bled at the same time.

You would be ashamed to see what I've let this house turn into. The house that you so carefully cleaned. You wouldn't recognize the place. I lie in my bedroom and feel the terrible weight of all the dank, untended rooms piled high with junk. My world is dark and heavy, the air thick with something, not just inside my home but in the street, the whole town, and farther and farther out so that even looking at the sky I never felt right, not even at the beach. Not when I said my marriage vows or when they put my first baby in my arms, or my second, or when my son said, "Ma, why don't you smoke a little grass to calm down"—this was thirty years ago—and I got high and felt the darkness and heaviness and disarray closing in on me, closer every minute, and I pictured the Four Horsemen of the Apocalypse coming for me, mainly just their horses, the relentless rush of hooves.

My mother had you pour tea for Nicholas when he came calling, weeks after the dance. Tea splashed over the lip of his cup and onto his pant leg.

"For heaven's sake, you're mindless," Mother said, and you ran to the kitchen for a towel.

While you were gone she whispered, "She's been so distracted lately. No thanks to you," and squeezed Nicholas's knee. "I suspect she has a crush."

Whenever Mother told a joke he threw his head back to laugh and I could see the gold tooth nested among his molars.

My father rose and put his heavy hand on top of my head. He suggested that Nicholas and I go for a walk. It was an absurd suggestion, as I'd been outside that morning and was greeted by cold that instantly froze my damp hair. Even inside the parlor the seam of the window let in a thin, needling slice of air.

"It's awful out there," I said.

"Now dear, why don't you just go along," said my mother, and she picked up her teacup and stared at it in fury like the steaming tea was my face. My father moved his hand from my hair to my shoulder.

"Never mind then," Nicholas said. He turned toward me on the couch, but looked beyond me to my parents. "The fact of it is I was hoping to ask you to be my wife."

It felt like a long pause but it was probably only seconds of silence in which I became aware that you'd been standing in the parlor doorway and had now disappeared from it.

There were a number of things I can think of that might have been held inside this moment. In hindsight I thought of my father on the day he got drunk with Nicholas, sitting on the stairs weeping as Nicholas played the piano and I sang. I thought of the sick way my father looked since Ben died, and of the warmth of his hand on my shoulder, a hand that squeezed my shoulder gently after Nicholas blurted his proposal, and less so, much less so, I thought of my mother, who had taken to wearing her robe from morning until evening, and ghosting around the house with her swollen eyes and mottled face. I thought of everyone laughing at the dance and Nicholas twirling you in his arms and the dance hall's circle of light, and how dark and cold it was as I walked back home alone, through the parlor where Mother was listening to Ben's old records and father was drinking scotch by the unlit fireplace, neither one of them noticing my bloody skirts or hand, and how cold my bed was at night before you crawled into it, the sound of Mother wailing through the walls, and

Nicholas's parents' fine house, with the polished silver, two maids, and bathtubs with golden taps, and his fine car. That is, I thought of Nicholas's money, but also I thought of packing his car with my things and moving away, to any place else, any place other than this one.

In this moment I didn't think any of those things. I just had a feeling, and I knew I would say yes.

"But what about Eva?" I said.

"Please," my mother said. "Eva's not the kind of girl you marry."

"That was just a bit of fun," said Nicholas, "while I waited for you. I wish her well. She understands that."

"This is what your brother would have wanted," my father said.

That night there were footsteps outside my door and I felt certain it was you but then in walked my mother, smelling of perfume though she wore her nightgown, a silk bundle in her arms. She sat beside me on the bed and smoothed back my hair.

"My little bride," she said. "I can't sleep I'm so excited. What are you thinking about?"

"Eva," I said.

"Now listen, she'll get over her schoolgirl crush." She began picking at a knot in my hair. "I'm letting Eva go at the end of the week. Your father and I won't need her anymore."

"You can't," I said. "Where will she go?"

"To her mother, I suppose. Leaving will do her good. People can only accept charity for so long before it makes them weak willed."

"Why don't Nicholas and I take her?" I said. "Nicholas has got enough money to keep her on. She's a good worker."

"Listen," my mother said. All the warmth of her face drained away leaving something cold and hard and revolted, though she continued to play with my hair. "Don't try to out-smart me. I'm not deaf and I'm not dumb." Her voice quieted to a hiss. "I've heard what you and that girl do. You've been very silly children and she is leaving." I didn't say anything. I didn't breathe.

"Now, I can't sleep until I see you in my dress," she said.

She stood behind me, adjusting the dress as I turned in front of the mirror. She kept telling me how beautiful I looked and I saw it was true. There was a knock on the door. You opened it and then retreated as soon as you saw my mother.

"Excuse me," you said.

"Not tonight, Eva," said Mother as you closed the door behind you.

It wasn't the end of the week when you left, but the next morning. Breakfast was not served at its usual time. Mother and Father watched as I hugged you goodbye on the porch, and in my memory I kissed you on the mouth, but I know that isn't right. You whispered in my ear, "Don't marry him," and I said aloud for the sake of those listening, "Safe travels," and we stood on the lawn and watched you walk away toward the train station. We could have arranged for a ride, but there was no time for all that, Mother said, with the wedding plans to be made. My father and mother went into the house and then my mother came back out to catch me crying. She slapped me and said, "Don't be so ungrateful. Of all the things I could have done, here I've given her half a chance to lead a respectable life. And you. This is a kindness."

There were many white steps leading to the church door. I wore Mother's silk slippers, and even though it was a warm day the marble held the cold, which seeped through their soles. I wore Mother's veil, a thick embroidered lace that draped over my head and came down to my ankles.

I've kept the wedding picture of Nicholas and me. I look handsome in the photograph. The veil ripples around my face. My hair is dark, and braided in a crown on top of my head. I am seventeen, and I look that young, but I don't look as nervous as one's supposed to look at seventeen. Nicholas, in the photo, could be called handsome. The cleft of his chin is a dark gash.

After the ceremony there was dinner in the dance hall—glazed geese and suckling pig with deflated eyes. The guests picked the bones clean, and danced and danced. I waltzed with my father, the musty wool of his tuxedo itching my cheek. Everyone stood outside the hall and waved goodbye as Nicholas and I drove away, tin cans clattering behind us.

The inn we drove to was very fine. It had silver taps in the bathroom. I took off my kid gloves. Sweat from my palms had turned their white satin trim gray. The hot water came gushing out so that I burned my hands. I rinsed my face and put on the gauzy nightgown my mother had picked out for me. It took me time to do up the many pearl buttons. I looked in the mirror, and my eyes were dark and darting, and my mouth was red. I thought about animals that will gnaw their foot off to get free from a trap, but I wasn't sure exactly what the trap was, in my case, or what being free was either. I was drunk. They had served pink champagne. There were many toasts. I took off my silk slippers. I washed my feet in the bathtub.

I thought Nicholas would have switched the lights out by the time I was done in the bathroom, but all the lights were on and he was lying naked on top of the covers. He was facing away from me, and I hoped he might be sleeping. He breathed with a catch in his throat, almost snoring. I climbed into bed as quietly as I could, shimmying under the tightly cinched sheet without untucking it.

He was stroking himself.

You must know what it is he did, as I must know what he did to you. It went on all night. I think it would have been easier in the dark, for then I would have been allowed the privacy of my face, its contortions. The bedside lamp made a buzzing noise—sometimes I couldn't hear it, sometimes it filled the room. There was a long, narrow watermark on the ceiling above the bed. He yanked my hair back, and positioned me in many different ways. It grew light outside.

When it was over, Nicholas was red and sore, and he handed me a wad of bills from the bedside table and told me to go to the store around the corner for balm. I didn't think I could walk, but I got up and walked to the bathroom and dressed. I could find only one faint bruise, already forming on my neck. There was only ever that one bruise. My lips were swollen, my chin rubbed raw from the stubble he had grown as the night drew on.

Perhaps he was gentler with me, if you can call what he did gentle, because I was the one he chose to take for a wife. Or perhaps, it strikes me now, you put up a fight, and I did not.

While I was at the store he ordered room service—poached eggs that wiggled when we shifted the table to sit in the patch of sun by the window. Fresh orange juice topped with a thick layer of pulp. I rubbed him quickly with the balm, before the eggs got cold. My wedding ring was too large for my finger, and the ointment made the band slick. It kept slipping past my finger's knuckle. I went to the bathroom feeling like I might throw up, but nothing happened, so I sat back down to breakfast. He went to pick up the car from the valet and to smoke. I washed myself and then the sheets with a bar of lavender-scented soap, but afterward I didn't know what to do with the sheets so I left them in a soggy heap in the bathtub and pulled the curtain closed.

On the curb, he handed me the wet stub of his cigar.

"I won't tell," he said. We passed it back and forth, and the sweet cigar made me dizzy. He winked at me, conspiratorial. He took my hand, and my nails pressed into his palm were part of the conspiracy, signaling the larger secret of what our bodies had done all night.

Our honeymoon was to consist of lots of driving, and lots of hotels. We left the inn and drove in silence. Even though it was nearly spring there had been a cold snap the night before, and there were ruts of ice in the road. Each time the car bumped over a rut the wheel slipped, out of control under his gloved hand, and I would gasp. He held the wheel loosely, like the car was an animal he had trained.

Finally, he pulled the car over to the shoulder and said, "How about you drive? I'll teach you."

I thought he was ribbing me, but he yanked the brake.

Nighttime in the next hotel room was fast approaching and I imagined taking the wheel and pressing the pedal to the floor, watching his face lose its half-smile as I drove us both off the road and into the river below. I got out of the car. The road was empty. No one to come along and help. Below us I could hear the river's violent rushing. In the driver's seat I strained my legs to reach the pedals and my legs started quaking and wouldn't stop. All night he'd held my legs spread in the air and now they didn't work anymore. Nicholas and I watched my legs as he explained how I should release the clutch as I gave it gas, "rock the baby," he called it, though I couldn't understand the analogy at all. And all the while the weak betrayal of my shaking legs.

"Look at that," he said. "Are you frightened?"

I shook my head and tried to press the pedal again and my leg shook and he snaked his hand under my skirt and up my thigh until it rested snugly between my legs.

"Come on," he coaxed. "Now gentle on the gas, ease it in. Rock the baby."

But I couldn't.

I don't know. Maybe if we'd both died that would have been better.

Nicholas was a body beside me his whole life long, and that brought me comfort. Whatever kind of man he was, I liked to watch the pulse in his neck as he slept, to have the living heat of him beside me in the bed. Other small comforts worked their way in too: the smell of his hair, or, when he held me, the itch of his wool lapel, which reminded me of my father. We had two children together, boys who looked just like him, and even from the beginning I loved recognizing Nicholas in their expressions. The terrible truth is that I wanted to hate him, I wanted to kill him, but from the moment my legs wouldn't let me start the car some part of me must have already begun the transformation from hating him to needing him.

And I did need him, as though his body working into mine all night and every night after that for forty years performed some secret alchemy that made me crave him—he who should have been sickening, he whom I wanted to repulse me. His smell, his hands, his neatly trimmed fingernails, even his breath, the taste of his skin, began to quicken something inside me that could not be slowed.

I got back into the passenger's seat and he started the car and we drove along. It was then I first began to let myself think about the truth of the matter: that all along Nicholas had quickened something in me, from the moment he leaned in drunkenly and snapped my book closed, and that my anger and aloneness over the dance and all of it was because I wanted him for myself. I wanted you both.

My hands were shaking in my lap. I was wet. I fingered the new, pink scar in the web between my pinky and ring finger and thought of you, or some hybrid of the two of us, pale with blurry features – dark mouthed, dark eyed, and shifty.

That night, the second night of our honeymoon, we stopped at an inn and the sun went down, and like the darkness signaled the start of a new world with newborn ways I buttoned up my nightgown in the bathroom and already it felt more familiar and comfortable than the night before. I got into bed beside Nicholas and curled up on my side but when he climbed on top of me, as I knew he would, I buried my face in his neck and clawed his back, and as he moved in me I still ached from the previous night, but it felt good, against my will, though I pretended it did not. The whole night long I did not permit myself to make a noise.

The Quarry

"We're white trash," said Valerie. Collette pushed her sunglasses to her forehead and squinted at her sister. Without the sepia-tinted lenses, the quarry and the distant swimmers looked too pale, unearthly.

"We're definitely not," Collette said. She glanced over to her mother Madge, who knelt on the gravelly patch that was their lawn, planting the plastic sandbox with petunias. "Think of Mom's dad. Didn't he meet the president once? And Mom got into Brown, even if she didn't want to go."

Valerie stretched out on her back, her hair splayed behind her, its tips trailing off the ledge into the water. Collette wondered if in five years, when she was fifteen, she would look anything like Valerie. Last summer, Valerie sunbathed in a purple bikini, and Collette peeled the sunburned skin from her back. But this summer Madge harassed Valerie into wearing a long white T-shirt over her bathing suit. Madge hadn't said anything about Collette having to cover herself, but she wore a baggy T-shirt anyway.

"We have two cars in the drive up on blocks," said Valerie. "Dad left before you ever met him. We have to eat that big, dumb brick of free cheese. Think about it, it doesn't go bad, like regular-people cheese. We live at the quarry. In Masonville. Seriously, can you think of anyone normal around here?" She gestured limply to Mr. Reed's double-wide, visible through the evergreens. The pinwheels on his lawn were whizzing. A half-deflated Santa, left over from Christmas, was doubled over, face down in the birdbath. Beside the birdbath, a claw-foot tub filled with dirt. Last summer Mr. Reed had paid them five dollars each to plant it with yellow carnations.

"That tub is no worse than Mom's sandbox," said Valerie.

"Stop," said Collette. She slapped her sister's thigh. "Mom can hear."

"So what if she does. She's been wearing that crop top everywhere, wearing it to the store, so no wonder everyone thinks we're trash even if we aren't."

"Well then your tooth makes us trash too," said Collette. Valerie had been clumsy when she was Collette's age, tripping down the front steps and knocking her mouth on the granite. Her canine chipped to a sharp point, and her front tooth turned gray from a dead root. Collette only noticed the dark tooth in certain lights or photographs, but sometimes Valerie would sit on the bathroom counter, looking in the mirror for up to an hour. Mornings she'd complain that the canine had pressed painfully into her cheek as she slept. Her teeth were the only flaw that Collette could see. Her sister's face was like her own, but somehow more, as though each feature had been amplified. Valerie's mouth was a bow, Collette's was wide and thin. Valerie's feet were high-arched, dancer's feet. Collette was flat footed. Valerie sang in a deep vibrato. Collette's voice was steady and high and plain, a peasant's voice.

"Go fuck yourself," said Valerie, quiet enough that Madge wouldn't hear, and Collette got up, smoothed her shirt, and walked to the water's edge. Far away a group of girls flailed around a raft, splashing each other. Up on the highest cliffs a crowd of men had parked their rusted-out pickups in a row. They set up lawn chairs to watch the girls swim. The seats of their chairs sagged from years of use.

"Lookin' good, ladies!" one of them shouted to the swimmers below, tossing an empty beer can off the cliff. Collette wondered if the men were looking at her and Valerie too, but she couldn't really tell. They were all wearing sunglasses.

Collette went back to Valerie, who had covered her face with her magazine.

"I can hear you breathing," said Valerie from underneath the glossy cover. "Would you move? You're blocking my sun."

Collette lifted the page's edge to kiss her sister on the forehead. Her hairline smelled like bananas from the sunscreen Madge had made them rub on before breakfast.

"I'm sorry I said that about your tooth," Collette said.

Valerie threw the magazine off her face and shrugged. Her cheeks were flushed.

"Lookin' good, girl," said Collette.

She rolled her eyes, unsmiling. "Whatever, you're forgiven. Give me your foot," she said, shaking the bottle of nail polish. Her tongue poked from the corner of her mouth as she painted Collette's nails. After one foot was done, she blew gently on each toe.

"Smelly feet," she said. "I'll paint your other foot tonight." She laid her cheek to the rock and closed her eyes.

"We could skip stones," said Collette.

"Nah," said Valerie.

"Please? I'll get them." She could see three flat stones in the shallow water, far enough from the drop-off that it was safe to wade. She kept her toes splayed so the polish wouldn't smudge and inched her feet into the cold. Her pink nails were like gems underwater. Her feet didn't seem like her own anymore, and for a while she was lost staring at them.

She took the smooth stones back to Valerie and lined them beside her. At first it looked like she was sleeping, but then her eyes opened.

"One of them is a wishing rock too," said Collette.

"I don't want to skip rocks. I'll try and teach you how later."

Collette traced the white line that wrapped around the rock with her finger. It made a complete ring, no breaks.

"You can have the wishing rock. What would you wish on it?'

"I'd wish to be free."

"Free to do what?"

"Free to lie here quietly."

Collette rubbed the rock against her nose. The oil darkened it, so it still looked wet.

"Free to swim," said Valerie.

"Well you can't have the wish, anyway," said Collette. "It doesn't work if you actually tell me."

"Like I care," said Valerie.

Collette put the stone in her T-shirt pocket. It hung there heavily. She had a collection of rocks like it in a giant clamshell on her bureau. She lifted her T-shirt again to press her stomach against warm granite. They lay in silence. The day was starting to cool. Mosquitoes buzzed at Collette's ears. The sun went behind clouds. Goose bumps cropped up over her body, she even felt them on the top of her head. She opened her eyes for a second to check that Valerie had them too.

"Come on inside," said Madge. "I'll make tuna sandwiches for dinner." She came down the pathway, and put a palm to Collette's neck, and then to Valerie's. Her hands were cold from digging in the dirt.

"I'll stay for a while," Valerie mumbled. "I'm having a dream."

"What are you dreaming about, baby?" said Madge. Collette stood and leaned on her mother's shoulder. Madge brushed a strand of hair from Collette's mouth.

"Underwater," Valerie said. "I swallowed a hook."

"Crazy talk," Madge whispered into Collette's ear.

"Mom, can't we swim this year? Please?" asked Collette. She had asked her mother at the start of every summer, when they pined the most for water. "Valerie really wants to swim."

"Do you want to catch a disease?"

Collette picked up a rock with her toes and threw it toward Madge's sandbox.

"A girl could catch herself a yeast infection just from swimming in this damn quarry." Collette looped her arms around Madge's neck. One of the men on the cliffs stood and poised to dive.

"I hope he has a death wish," Madge said. Collette knew about the dangers of diving, how old machinery or a jagged outcropping of rock could be hidden just out of view, and she knew about the dangers of disease, how homeless travelers came to bathe in the summer, how drunk men would unzip their flies and arc their piss into the water from high up on the embankment. Beyond the shallow ledge it was deep, fifty feet, maybe a hundred. She didn't know for sure. So much snow melted each spring, and raised the water level, leaving the water icy below the surface warmth.

Later Collette licked her finger to pick up potato chip crumbs, and looked out the kitchen window as Valerie rose and stretched, touching one foot and then the other, like a superstitious pitcher with a ritual. She tested the stone's weight in her hand before skipping it across the water. Collette fogged the window, counting the ten skips under her breath.

*　*　*

"Tell me the story," said Collette. She flipped the pillow under her head to the cool side. Valerie was sitting up in the bed next to Collette's, trying on her many rings. Outside their wide storm window the quarry lay in the darkness, flat as a rug against the granite shoreline. Collette could see a fissure of moonlight moving over the surface.

"Well, I wasn't going to say anything, but I saw something swimming under the water when we were sunbathing. It didn't look human."

"Don't make fun," said Collette. "I know the stories aren't real. I just want to hear one tonight." Valerie twisted her dark hair and anchored it in a bun at her neck, so it would curl in the morning.

"This is my story. Do you want to know what it looked like or not?"

Collette nodded, and moved closer to the wall so her back pressed against it.

"It came out of the darkness. I only saw it for a second. It had eyes that were clouded over, like marbles. Its skin was translucent. It was like a human, but with long thin feet and fingers, for swimming swiftly." It was the same creature she always described, slimy and gray. Collette pulled the blanket up to her neck. "You were wading in the shallows when I saw it, but by the time I tried to warn you it was gone again. You've got nothing to worry about though. Everyone knows the creature can only climb out of the water at night, when the sky is clear and you can see the moon. Only on nights like tonight. And now it's time for you to go to bed."

"How does it move on land?" asked Collette, but she knew the answer. It slithered, like a snake.

"Do you see it?" Collette shouted out in the early morning. "Do you see it?"

"Jesus Christ, Collette," said Valerie. "What's your problem?" The room was empty and clean, lit with the cold light of early morning. Dawn was windless, and the water outside was smooth. "I thought someone was in here." Collette couldn't remember what she had dreamed.

The bathroom door stuck when Collette tried to open it. "Stay out!" Valerie shouted, but Collette went in anyway. The bubbles in Valerie's bath had popped and the soap formed a skin on the surface of the water, the rounds of Valerie's knees all that were visible of her body. As recently as that winter, Collette had been allowed to sit on the edge of the tub while Valerie lathered her hair, and they would talk about school. Collette would glance at her naked sister, trying to learn something about what her own woman's body would someday look like. Valerie had shown Collette how she shaved, drawing the razor over her legs twice, holding it under the tap to rinse flecks of hair clean from the blade. Collette wasn't allowed to shave yet, but Valerie would let her practice putting on shaving cream and running the backside of the razor up her legs, never above the knee. Madge always said there was no need for a girl to shave above the knee.

Collette's leg hair was blonde and thin. She didn't want shaved legs, but she liked the minty-clean smell of the shaving cream, and the way it made her skin tingle afterward.

"Collette, please, out!"

"I just wanted to brush my teeth," Collette said. "You've been in here for an hour."

"I'm putting a lock on this door," said Valerie.

Collette put a streak of toothpaste on the brush, not bothering to squeeze from the bottom of the tube like she was supposed to. She brushed her teeth in the hallway, harder and longer than usual, until foam spilled from the corners of her mouth and she couldn't help but swallow it.

"Mom," Valerie yelled over the sucking sound of the drain. "Can I spend the night at Jill's?" She opened the door and the smell of her coconut shampoo drifted into the hallway.

"I'm working the night shift," said Madge.

"Can't Mr. Reed babysit until you get home?"

"No, come on, guys," Collette said. "I'm not a little kid. I'll be fine alone." Valerie blocked the hallway. She snapped her neck up and down, flicking her hair in an arc, speckling Collette's face with droplets of water.

"It's not fair to ask him on such late notice," said Madge.

"You kidding? He loves it. Gives him something to do," Valerie said.

Madge flipped a Mickey Mouse–shaped pancake. "He probably has plans for his Saturday night."

"Please, Mom. He's like, forty. No one has plans when they're forty. You've seen his TV glowing when you get in late from work. He's an insomniac. He'll be up. Please, please? Jill's dad is making pizza."

Madge shook her head and dialed Mr. Reed. The screen door hit the back of Collette's legs as she went outside. The rocks she collected were hot, and she skipped them hard into the water. They splashed in and quickly sank.

Collette was reading Goosebumps on the couch, her cheek propped in her hand and her pinky falling asleep, when she nodded off. When she woke up the sounds of the house were different. Valerie's stomping and her long, shaking sighs were gone, and so was the sound of Madge shuffling in bedroom slippers. She could hear someone digging around inside a crinkling bag, and she opened her eyes. Mr. Reed sat in the armchair, eating caramel corn. He put one piece into his mouth at a time, and Collette imagined that he ate them like she did, letting the kernel dissolve on his tongue without chewing. It must have been past midnight, because Collette knew that's when *X-Files* came on. Collette had seen this episode before, where an alien came lurching out of the woman's stomach and latched its mouth onto the man beside her. She'd watched it in Madge's bedroom with Valerie, all three of them unable to sleep and staring at the screen through the spread of their fingers. Collette didn't want to watch this part again. She closed her eyes. Mr. Reed got up and ran the tap. The screams from the television rose until the show cut to a commercial break. Collette began to dream that she was sliding down a very long banister, so fast that when she reached the bottom the banister behind her was on fire.

It wasn't until he was very close that she realized Mr. Reed had come back into the room, had crouched down beside the couch and was holding his fingers just above her chest, the space between his fingers and her skin tingling and warm. She was wearing an old soccer jersey of Valerie's, and Collette was aware now that the shirt hung off one of her shoulders. She told herself that she was imagining things, but the air smelled buttery with his breath, and then she heard the creak of his joints, and the sound of him moving, ever so carefully, against the shag carpet as he rocked to the balls of his feet. On the television a woman talked about a powder that would make your face look airbrushed. Collette tried to focus on the woman's voice, to bring her heart back into rhythm, but the other sounds, the human sounds of the body beside her, were too loud. She could hear his stomach gurgling, his tongue shifting inside his mouth. *Keep your eyes closed*, Collette thought. She realized she was holding her breath, and tried to inhale secretly. *Keep breathing*. Then his fingertips were on her, lightly, very gently, almost not there at all. As soon as he had touched her he was gone from her side. He cleared his throat, turned down the volume on the TV, creaked back into the armchair. Collette could still feel his calloused fingers grazing her skin and then drawing quickly back as though she had burned him.

* * *

91

"Why do I have to go to bed?" said Collette. "Valerie gets to stay up." Splashes came from the bathroom where Valerie soaked and soaked inside the tub. She was singing softly to herself from behind the door.

"Valerie is five years older than you. And Valerie doesn't have bags under her eyes, like you do." Collette drew a finger under each eye. The skin there felt puffy.

"Fine," said Collette. She walked down the hall to Madge's bedroom. The bed was made, and Collette pulled back a corner of the covers and slipped under.

There were two pictures on Madge's nightstand, one of Collette and one of Valerie. Collette switched them so that hers was angled closer toward the bed. In the picture she was playing dress up, wearing Madge's dress. The dress trailed on the ground behind her, and she held a parasol. She had her hair in a style she used to insist on, that Madge deemed "The Unicorn"—one ponytail right above her forehead.

Madge rapped at the door and Collette pulled the sheet over her face.

"I just want to stay in here," said Collette from under the sheet.

"You have a nice room of your own," said Madge. The bed shifted as she sat down beside Collette.

"I know Valerie used to sleep in here all the time, when she was little."

"She slept in my bed when she was four. Dad had just left. She needed to sleep down here for a while. You're ten."

Madge peeled back the sheet. "What's your excuse?" She stroked Collette's cheek with the back of her hand.

"Never mind. I'll just watch TV in here with you for a while."

"Sweetie, you look so tired. It's time to go to bed. I'll heat you some milk." Collette could feel her chin threatening to wobble, so she pressed her face to the pillow and nodded. She didn't move until Madge came back from the kitchen. The mug burned her hands. She had to hold it carefully by the handle.

"What's got you sad?" Madge said. Collette shrugged. She held the mug in front of her mouth.

"Will you tell me?" said Madge. Collette shrugged again. "Go on up, then. Sweet dreams. It'll feel better tomorrow."

"Sweet dreams," said Collette. She left Madge's room and stood in the hallway, in front of the bathroom door, blowing on the steaming milk for a few minutes. She put her hand on the bathroom doorknob, turning it very slowly so that Valerie wouldn't notice from the other side. It was still locked. Valerie had gone to the hardware store to buy the lock herself, had installed it without saying anything to Collette.

"Goodnight," Collette said to the crack of light coming from the seam in the door.

"Goodnight," Valerie said. "Weirdo."

Upstairs, the bedroom was quiet and too hot. A spider crawled across the floor, and Collette searched for something to kill it with. She grabbed one of Valerie's magazines and snuck up on the spider, which had frozen in its path. She slapped it hard once. When she pulled the magazine up, its legs had curled in on itself but they were still moving.

"I'm really sorry," she said, "sorry, sorry, sorry," with each slap of the magazine. The broken pieces of spider stuck to the magazine's cover. She slid them into the wastebasket with the end of a pen.

Collette undressed under her blanket, changing into one of Madge's vintage nightgowns. It had frills on the collar and round pearl buttons down the front. She got up to close the curtains, keeping her eyes on the reflection of the room in the window and not the quarry beyond it. She was in bed when she noticed the closet door was open. She got up again to close the door, but left it slightly ajar to show whatever she was afraid of that she was not really so afraid. Then she adjusted the bedroom door, making sure it was angled exactly with the knot in the pine floorboard. The milk had grown a skin, and she didn't want it anymore.

She wrapped her sheet tightly around her, pulled the collar of Madge's nightgown over her mouth. One pillow went behind her, and she held Mr. Rabbit to her chest.

Sometime after she fell asleep she woke up startled, and in the darkness could make out the shape of Valerie standing naked before the mirror, her back to Collette. The air smelled like bubble bath. When Collette's eyes adjusted to the dark of the room, she saw the clean stripe across Valerie's back. It was a tan line. The pale outline of skin in the dark made it look like Valerie was wearing a bikini. She turned toward

Collette, as though she'd known she was being watched. She had smudges under her eyes where mascara had bled. Her eyes were shining. She put a finger to her lips.

Collette liked to turn over rocks in the woods, to watch what was underneath scuttle down into the earth. She was looking for a salamander, black with yellow spots. She found a daddy longlegs, a fragile lattice of moss, and mealy bugs that scattered. When she overturned a piece of rotten wood the salamander was there, its tail stuck up in the air in fear. It didn't run from her, and she laid her hand down beside it, palm up, and waited, hoping it would forget it was afraid.

Its feet were sticky as it walked onto her palm, and its skin was sleek and slippery. The woods around her smelled like the inside of a greenhouse. This was Collette's favorite smell.

There were people laughing up on the quarry cliffs, but Collette didn't move to see them, and she didn't want them to see her. She was holding the salamander very still, and she put her other hand gently over it, leaving a hole between her fingers so she could be sure it was still breathing. A long time passed before it went still in her hands. The trees around her cracked, sounds that came from deep inside their trunks. She eased the salamander into a cleaned spaghetti jar with holes poked through the lid. The voices up on the ridge rose. Collette put the jar in her backpack, leaving the top unzipped so it wouldn't get too hot inside. The pine needles that covered the ground had pressed into her knees, and when she brushed them off the grooves in her skin looked like fingernail marks.

She heard it clearly then, Valerie's laughter. Valerie's laughter was carrying over the water, through the line of trees that separated the woods Collette explored from the quarry cliffs.

Madge was at work at the restaurant, with Valerie left to babysit. When Collette snuck off to play in the woods that morning, Valerie was dozing outside on the rocks, her feet in the water, the sleep lines from her sheets still imprinted on her shoulders. Collette almost left her a note, but she liked the idea of Valerie walking through the woods, her gaze searching between the tall pines for Collette, the sound of Collette's name being called quietly at first and then louder.

But Valerie was not looking for her. Valerie was laughing, and her laughter came from the cliffs where Madge did not allow them to go. Collette kept low and climbed closer, to the bank where the woods overlooked the quarry. She ducked behind a tree that had fallen onto its side, the roots making a wall she could peek over.

And there was Valerie, on one of the lower ledges, one you had to jump to get to. It looked like the kind of jump that hurt your ankles when you landed. She was crouched at the edge of the rock, her hands arrowed in the direction of the quarry. She wore the purple bikini, and her head was bent down to her chest so her black hair hung over her face. A man crouched behind her, in a pair of swimming trunks and a white T-shirt. He had his hand on the small of Valerie's back. He was showing her how to dive.

Even stooped over as he was, Collette could tell the man was Mr. Reed. He was lanky and tall, with ears that stuck out, dark eyebrows, a wide smile. His curled brown hair was thinning on top and cropped close to his neck. He had a wrinkle there, where the skin sunburned two crisp lines. He pressed Valerie's head down, stretching her hands longer in front of her.

"This is how you do it," Collette heard him say. He stood and took his shirt off. He was skinny, with softness above his hips and tight curls of hair across his chest. Valerie sat back, looking up at him, her legs dangling off the ledge. Her cheeks were red and shiny, and she was smiling, shielding her eyes. He got into the diving position again, then tipped forward into the water. His hands cut the surface first, his body arrowed in after. Collette watched his shape swim down deep, then emerge through the green murk, eyes squinched tightly closed.

He reached his hands up out of the water, planted them on the slab of rock between Valerie's thighs, and lifted himself from the quarry, landing on top of her. Collette couldn't see her sister anymore, only the dripping shape of Mr. Reed that covered her body. Valerie's hair spilled out behind them.

"Hey!" Collette was about to shout, "Leave her alone!" when she heard Valerie say, clearly, "John." Neither of them had called Mr. Reed John before. Collette watched as Valerie's hand wrapped itself around the back of Mr. Reed's neck, tugging gently, pulling him closer.

OK, she thought, as she walked through the woods back to the house, *it's OK, everything is going to be all right*. She mouthed the thought to herself.

But when she got to her house, she took off her backpack and realized her mistake. She had leaned too long on the zippered opening while she watched Valerie. She had forgotten about the salamander. *Of course*, she thought, pulling the warm jar from her backpack. The jar had turned upside down on her walk back to the house, and her salamander lay near the lid, the tension in its limbs gone lax.

There was a burn in the back of her throat that would not go away. She didn't want to touch the salamander anymore. Its eyes were still open, and she picked it out of the jar with a pair of tongs from the kitchen. She laid it on Valerie's pillow. It curled in on itself like a tiny black snake.

That night Collette waited for Valerie to pull back her covers and find the salamander. It was dark when Valerie came into the room and slid into bed. She rested her head on the pillow without noticing anything, and soon she breathed heavily, sleeping.

"Valerie," Collette said into the dark. As soon as she spoke she wished she could take it back. Valerie shifted, sighed.

"What?" she said. "What's wrong?"

"Please don't be mad," Collette said, trying to keep her voice from shaking, "But there's a thing on your pillow."

Valerie switched on the table lamp. Her reaction was just as Collette had envisioned, squealing, pillow flung across the room.

"What the hell was that," yelled Valerie, her face twisted.

"I'm sorry."

"You are so retarded." Then Valerie was standing above Collette, hitting her with a feather pillow. The force of her hand came through the padding of the pillow, pummeling Collette's nose.

"You're a bitch," screamed Collette. She screamed louder than she had intended but the scream was lost in the press of the pillow against her mouth. "Ow, stop, stop, stop," Collette said. Valerie pulled back but Collette kept on saying it. Her body was quaking with sobs. She pressed her face into the pillow so Valerie couldn't look at her.

"OK, OK," Valerie was saying. She squeezed Collette's shoulder, not unkindly. "Did I actually hurt you? Are you really hurt?" Collette shook her head no, and then she knew that she was going to say it, that she had to say it, that it was too late not to.

"I saw you with Mr. Reed." Valerie's hand dropped from Collette's shoulder.

"I saw you with him," Collette said, trying to catch her breath. "And I saw how you liked it. And I know that you've been wearing a bikini, and that you've been swimming in the quarry with him."

"You're not going to tell Mom."

"I saw how you touched him," said Collette. "Maybe I am going to tell Mom. Will you stop? If you stop I won't tell Mom."

"Sure," said Valerie, the word quick and sharp. "I'll stop."

"Please, I'm not kidding," Collette said. "He probably doesn't even like you." Valerie didn't say anything, just stared at her. "He does bad things."

"What?" Valerie said, shaking her head. "I knew it. What, he touched you or something?"

"Just trust me," said Collette. She held Mr. Rabbit to her face, rubbing the worn fuzz of his ear against her lip.

"I'll bet he touched you," Valerie said. She got up from Collette's bed and stood over her, arms crossed, shifting her weight from one foot to the other.

"You better tell me," Valerie said. "Did you do something with him?"

"I didn't do anything," said Collette. "I was just sleeping. I was just sleeping on the couch."

"Goddamn him," Valerie said. "I knew it." She went back to her own side of the room and cracked the window. The room was quickly cold.

"You knew?" said Collette, holding Mr. Rabbit to her face, breathing him in. He smelled like their house, like smoke from the woodstove and the rosewater that Madge sprinkled in with the bedding when she washed it. "I don't want to be your sister anymore," she said.

"That's fine with me," said Valerie. She was almost smiling. "But tell Mom, tell anyone, and I'll leave. I'm serious. You won't know where I'm going. He wants to leave with me. If you tell, I won't have any reason to stay."

"Fine," said Collette. "Forget about it. I'm not telling." She lay in bed and forced herself to think nice things about Valerie. How Valerie used to pick her up and carry her on her shoulders, how afraid of falling Collette had been. They would walk the quarry roads until Collette grew comfortable with the height. Or before school, how Valerie used to French braid Collette's hair, her hands tugging roughly. She would sleep for days with the braid in.

"Do you love him or something?" Collette asked.

"It's none of your business if I love him," said Valerie. "So just let it go." But after a few minutes Valerie cleared her throat.

"Yeah, he loves me."

"Yeah?"

"What he did with you, that's just his way. It's got nothing to do with you. It doesn't mean anything."

"I guess he didn't touch me, really," said Collette. "He only acted like he might have wanted to."

"You shouldn't lie about things you don't know about."

"I didn't lie."

"Sure you didn't," Valerie said, climbing back into her bed, hugging her pillow like it was a person.

"What's it like?" Collette asked.

"What's what like?" said Valerie.

"Mr. Reed," said Collette. "He's so old."

"He's not all that old."

"Well, old compared to us. What's it like that he loves you, I guess."

"He's familiar, I don't know. We've known each other a long time," said Valerie.

"Why didn't you tell me?" They were both quiet. "Do you two see each other a lot? Where do you go?"

"Jesus, Collette," said Valerie, punching the pillow. "You really don't want to know this stuff, so I don't know why you're asking."

"Sure I do."

"No, you don't."

"I do." Collette's nose was running. She wiped it on the sleeve of her nightgown.

"You want everything? You want to know all my business?"

"Just something," she said. "Just asking."

"Yeah, OK," said Valerie. "Here's the really good stuff." She sat up in bed. "Before school let out, sometimes he'd pick me up after class and we'd drive to this graveyard, and he'd park the car in the weeds by the old part, where no one goes. The first time we went up there, he told me he would teach me driving on the logging roads, but I could barely steer. There were so many weeds grown up in the center of the lane, and the tires spun in the mud. I had on peppermint lip balm, and he leaned over me to take the wheel in his hands, and he told me the smell of me was making him crazy. And then we made love. At first I was scared, you know, but he knows a lot of things I didn't know, and he's good. He moved my hands for me. At first, the first few times, I would just lay there in the seat and let him do what he wanted. He has those two gross Newfoundlands, you know? Dog hair was all over the ceiling of the car. I was nervous back then, but he was so gentle to me. That's how I knew he might love me, there were clues. He would hold me after, and sometimes I would see him standing outside school during the day, just watching the windows for me. And then he told me that I grounded something in him, that when he wasn't around me for a few days his hands would shake, like withdrawal. And I think about him all the time too now, lying in that car together, how heavy he is on top of me, how nice it is to be on top of him—"

"That's OK," said Collette. "Thanks for telling me. I don't need to know."

"The first time it hurt, of course, like they all say, we didn't fit together at first and once we did there was a little blood, but now it doesn't hurt."

"Stop," Collette said. "Never mind. I don't need to hear any more."

"You made me tell you all my business so I'm going to tell you."

"Please stop," said Collette.

"I can still feel him inside me," hissed Valerie.

Collette pulled the pillow up over her ear.

"You wanted me to tell you about my love life like sisters do, but I can't tell you anything, I should have realized, because you're a baby."

Collette tried the tricks that Madge had taught her for falling asleep. Take all your worries and picture blowing them into a large balloon, then tie the balloon off and let it go, watch it rise into the clouds far above you and away. Or tense each part of your body, then relax them one by one, until everything is relaxed: your tongue, your eyelids, the joints of your toes.

In the morning, Valerie was gone.

The makeup was missing from her vanity. Half of the hangers in her closet were empty.

"Where's your sister?" Madge asked at eleven. She had just come in from the garden. Her hands were covered in dirt and she was trying to wipe an itch off her nose with her arm.

"Dunno," said Collette. She went into the bathroom, and locked the door. She brushed her teeth and then her tongue, gagged. She washed her face with Valerie's soap, scrubbing the stiff cloth against her cheeks until they burned red. The bathwater was scalding. She soaked all afternoon.

Glow Baby

The lion tucked me in each night. One night I couldn't look at the lion, so I looked at Mom, who bared her teeth as she spoke in his low growl. I told her I was scared to sleep with him.

"Why are you telling her?" the lion said, taking my earlobe in his mouth. I could feel the warmth of her arm through the fur of his body, and her fingers inside him, gently pinching my ear. "My girl. You're lucky I love you, or else I'd eat you."

"I don't want to play anymore," I said, and started to cry. The lion fell into her lap. She pulled her hand free and untangled a knot in his mane.

"What do you want me to do, Scoob?" she said. I asked her to hide him, but to tell me where he was hiding. When I closed my eyes her hand tunneled under my mattress. "OK," she said. "You can open."

All night I lay awake imagining the lion's body between the mattress and the box spring, crushed by my weight. I got out of bed and tried to lift the corner of the mattress but it was too heavy and too dark to see him. When I reached in I found crumbs and the outlines of springs, and a small, thin shape that turned out to be a pencil stub. I put the pencil stub under my pillow. The sky turned pink. Mom came running in, naked. She braced herself in the doorway, her eyes barely open.

"What's happening?" she said, and I said nothing was happening.

"I thought I heard screaming." I hadn't been screaming, and was mad at her for running in naked and making a big deal. She sat down beside me on the bed and held my hand. Her blonde braid was matted and her hand shook. I told her if she was cold she could get under my covers, even though dark hair covered her legs. I was afraid of her legs touching mine.

"Did you have a nightmare?" she said.

"All I was doing was being awake."

I told her I couldn't find Lion under the bed. He must be hiding from me, she said, in the farthest corner. Because he was more afraid of me than I was of him.

"Please," I said. "Find him."

"Only if you really want him."

I closed my eyes and hugged him. I pretended to myself that I still loved him, because if I didn't he might get back at me.

"Don't leave," I said.

"I'm right here." But her voice was already across the room.

The diaper was three years old, and it was too small. The plastic stretched to fit my hips. When I worked my finger between the diaper and my thigh there was a red groove already in my skin. I ripped the leg holes wider. I thought I might pee the bed, even though I hadn't peed the bed in years.

I climbed on the stove for the cookies hidden from me in the upper cabinet and ate one whole sleeve with six cookies, and then I wasn't hungry but I ate six more and put six in my bathrobe pocket. I turned the heat all the way up and sat by the vent until my fingers tingled. Dad's banjo was propped against the couch from when he sang to us about catching catfish, and rain. "Hi," I said, into the banjo's strings. "Good morning." When Mom fought with Dad the banjo rang from her shouting, and afterward it became a joke between them. I shouted, "Hi," but the banjo didn't make any noise.

"Jesus H. Christ." Mom stomped down the stairs, trailing a blanket. "We're roasting. Isn't it funny, I'm afraid in my own house that your dad is going to come home and catch us with the heat on." I climbed into her lap. "I'm always feeling like he's going to catch me," she said.

*   *   *

"Can't you have another baby?"

I held a clump of her hair in my mouth, waiting to braid it. She didn't say anything.

"I just want a sister," I said. "I'm lonely."

"Scoob, cut me a break."

"I want a family."

"Be gentle," she said.

I concentrated on the braid. Her hair was as long as her spine, which I could see through her T-shirt, and the braid would cover it up.

"That's nice," she said.

"Your hair smells," I said.

I wanted to take it back. Her hair was soft and blonde, full of static when I brushed it. Instead I said "Why are you so ugly?"

I drew a picture of her in my notebook with hair down to the ground that curled at the ends and started growing upward. Her bedroom door was locked. I lay down and slid the picture under the door. She didn't pick the picture up but must have seen it, because I heard her start to cry. I put my fingers under the door and held them there.

She touched my fingers with her toes.

"Come down," I said, and a sliver of blue bathrobe appeared, and then there was the light of her eye, blinking back at me.

"Can't you just let me alone for a while?" she said.
"Why?"

"Because I don't feel good."

"Do you want ginger ale?"

"I don't know what I want."

When I got back I knocked and knocked on her door until finally she opened it.

She wore Dad's orange hunting hat. "Oh God, don't look at me," she said, flopping down on the bed, laughing, wiping at her eyes. She covered her face with her hands. "I'm in trouble now." I lay alongside her and snatched the hat from her head.

"Please," she said, smacking my hand but it was too late. Her hair was gone.

Her head looked tiny without it, her ears too big. There were patches on her head where scalp showed through. I buried my face in her neck, hiding from her.

"We're OK," she said, rubbing my back. "It's just hair. I am not my hair." I was crying. I hated her. I bit her.

"Ow, you little asshole." She yanked up her sleeve to show me the tooth marks.

I ran away, kicking the ginger ale. I peed into the diaper. I rubbed my bedroom carpet until my palms were black. The carpet hid strands of my loose hair, and Mom's, and I collected it, hiding with the tuft of hair under my bed. One of Mom's dangly earrings was stuck between the floorboards, and I tucked it, along with a wooden giraffe, into the center of the hair, as though it was their nest.

*   *   *

"Scoob?" said Mom. "It's time to come out." Her fingertips grazed my sleeve.

"That's not my name," I said. "Don't call me that."

"What should I call you?"

"Mildred."

"Milly, trust me," she said. "That's an old lady name."

"Then why'd you name me it?"

"To burden you," she said. "Come here."

I scooched closer and touched the thin, scabbed line of blood behind her ear. "Look," I said.

"But it's my own head." She rolled her eyes around and twisted her neck like she was trying to look.

Her hair was curled inside her bathroom sink. I gathered it in my arms. I expected it to be pale yellow, but now it looked duller and darker. It was warm.

The cold came streaming in with Dad. "It's a world out there," he said. He lifted the pot off the stove and wiggled the jellied can-shaped blob of tomato soup. "What's this delicacy?"

I climbed on the counter to clean the snow from his eyebrows and beard.

"Feet off that counter," he said.

"They're clean."

"As if." He tickled them. I screamed and screamed until I couldn't breathe. "Let's conduct an experiment." He took my hand and rubbed my palm with his thumb. A dark pill of dirt appeared and he picked it up and held it in front of my face. "Evidence," he said. "Tell Mom, bath time after dinner."

She came into the doorway with a flowered scarf wrapped around her head.

"Hey, sweeties," she said, running the scarf's long tail through her fingers. "Do you like it?"

"What's to like?" said Dad.

"It's terrible," she said.

"Did you cut it? I'm sure it's lovely."

"It's not."

"It's lovely," I said.

She untied the scarf.

"Oh, Carla," said Dad.

Mom stood in the doorway, smiling and then not. "Well aren't you going to say anything?" she said. She smiled again. Dad looked at her, and then he looked at me. The soup started to smoke.

At dinner Mom wouldn't look at either of us. She spooned soup into her mouth even though it was too hot to eat.

"I do like it," said Dad. "It's gamine. Very Twiggy."

"Can't we say grace?" I said.

"Since when do we say grace?"

"I think we used to."

He raised his beer bottle. "Hear, hear. We're a family."

I asked for a sip of his beer. "Don't develop a taste for it," he said.

"No way," Mom said.

"No harm in a sip. She's not a baby."

"She is a baby."

The beer was bitter, like when I'd filled my mouth with pennies from the change jar. I had three swallows before Mom grabbed the bottle, spilling beer across my nightgown.

"Well, if she's a baby why not give her a bath once in a while?" Dad said. "She stinks. What's that about?"

"What a horrible thing to say," said Mom. "She doesn't stink."

"I smelled her as soon as I walked in," he said.

I could feel the diaper's weight, soggy and stinking. I could smell it now that he said it.

"You're shaming her."

"Please," Dad said. She took my hand and led me up the stairs. "Carla," he called after us. "All I'm saying is we need to take care of each other."

"I can do it myself," I said as she pulled off my nightgown for the bath. "Don't look." I turned away.

"Honey pie," she said. She frowned, running her thumb over the diaper's band. "What is that? You don't need that." I pulled the diaper off. There were red lines on my hips and thighs.

"I just wanted to wear one," I said. "I have bad dreams."

The bathwater burned my legs but I got in anyway and she soaped my hair, tugging through the knots. When she pulled her hands away my hair was all over her fingers. She held her hands out in front of her.

"I'm so sorry," she said. "Soap yourself. You're a big girl."

The soap slipped from my hands, down into the scummy bathwater. I was afraid to put my head underwater to rinse my hair, but I lay back and put my ears under. I could hear Mom's voice, like a long, wide tunnel digging toward me underground.

The house went quiet and the bathwater cold. The hallway was dark. I went downstairs to the kitchen and lay next to Olive on her dog bed. I put my head on her stomach and listened to its gurgling. She looked at me like she was in trouble. She licked my hand. "You're OK," I said.

When I woke up someone was standing by the kitchen door.

"Hello?" I said.

Mom made a strange kind of yelp. My eyes found her face in the dark. Her coat glistened.

"Shhhhh," she whispered. "What are you doing here?"

"What are you?" I said.

"Be very quiet. Olive will bark."

She sat next to me on the dog bed, pulling me into her lap. Her hands were the coldest I'd ever felt skin be. She kissed my cheek, and I pulled away.

113

"Please," she said. "Just let me give you one kiss."

"Where were you?"

"Just out," she said.

"Aren't you going to sleep?" I traced my finger along the vine stitched up her coat's sleeve.

"I napped a little, down at the dock. It's warm in the boathouse."

"You can't sleep there."

"But I do," she said. I tried to match my breathing to hers, but she breathed too fast. Her eyes were closed. "Some grown-ups don't need too much sleep," she said. "Let's just be quiet for a little while." She kissed the top of my head. She was crying into my hair. "Oh, I love your smell," she said. "I'm going to ask you a question and don't worry about the answer. Just say what you want. I need to go away for a while, and you can stay with Dad, or you can come with me."

"With you," I said, as fast as I could.

"I don't know," she said. "Dad will miss you."

"Don't go," I said. I started to cry.

"Can we make a deal, OK? This is the condition of you coming along. On this trip, I'm not Mom. Just for this trip. I'm your best friend, think of it that way."

Olive stood up with us and jingled her tags. "Stay," Mom hissed.

The car radio was already on, playing static. The wheels spun out down the snowy drive.

"Don't look," she said, so I did, and there was Dad in his white bathrobe in the doorway of the house, growing small behind us. He ran out, barefoot in the snow, Olive behind him, barking.

"He's fine," she said. "He's just saying goodbye."

"I want Olive."

"Dad needs her."

We sped out of town, the wheels sliding. On the main road, thick fog lined the ditches.

"But you're my mom," I said.

"I know, Scoob."

"I like you as my mom."

"You're just too little to understand I'm terrible."

"I'm not too little," I said.

"Fine, you're not too little."

"I hate you."

"That's rude, but fine. That's good. You're good at this."

A tape played a song about a woman riding down a desert highway on a Harley-Davidson, her long hair blowing behind her. I imagined a Harley-Davidson was a kind of horse. I held the curl of Mom's loose hair in my pocket. It felt like the dry tip of a paintbrush. She bought a soda too giant for the cup holder. It sloshed between my knees. "Where are we going?" I said. "Where are we going? Where are we going?"

At the mall she locked the doors.

"I'll be back before you notice I'm gone," she said. "Can I get you anything?"

"Just this doll I saw on TV is all," I said. "It has a button that makes it glow. It's called a Glow Baby."

"I'd want that too," she said.

I hid under her coat, rubbing the red silk lining against my cheek. After what felt like too long there was a knock at the window. She cupped her hands to the glass, peering in.

"Open up." Her long hair was back and instead of jeans and a sweater she wore a blue kimono. She cradled a baby doll.

"A wig, see?" she said, slipping off her hair. "Unlock, please." My breath fogged the glass. "Touch it," she said. She threw the yellow hair into my lap. "Good, huh? Real.

"No such luck with the Glow Baby. This one was the best of the bunch."

I searched the doll's back for a button anyway, and then untied her dress and bonnet. She didn't even have eyes that opened and closed when I moved her head up and down. I squeezed her stomach and it stayed indented.

"Look," I said.

"Don't do that to her."

I put her dress back on, and her hat, and tried to get the dent out of her stomach but it was stuck that way.

Mom adjusted her wig in the rearview mirror. She had her old face back, the way it used to be. "It looks just like you," I said.

We waited in the cold on her friend's stoop, ringing the bell every few minutes until we saw him on the other side of the door. He looked at us through rippled glass.

Mom called, "It's Carla."

"Who?" He fumbled with the lock.

"It's Carla and Milly," she said.

He opened the door a few inches. "Carla." The man smiled and shook his head. "What are you doing here? This is great." He pulled me into their hug. "Let me look at you." His big hands cupped Mom's face, turning it left and right. "It's been too long. What a surprise."

"You have a weird accent," I said.

"And look at this face. You've delivered me an angel." He tugged on my chin. "I'm sorry I had you wait, come in, please, I was in the shower. What is this treat?" He took Mom's coat from my arms. "You must be freezing, left waiting so long," he said. "Water? Wine?"

"You know me," Mom said. He poured two glasses of wine. I'd never seen her drink wine.

"Hot chocolate for you, Milly?" To Mom he said, "Look at this enormous creature."

I shrugged.

"Be nice to my friend, Milly," she said.

"How do you even know him?"

"We danced together, in college."

"You don't dance," I said.

"She does so," he said. "Your mother's a very talented girl."

"Girl, hardly," Mom said.

"You're still a girl," he said. "You're still beautiful."

He forgot to stir the chocolate syrup into the milk, so I drank the hot milk and then the syrup. The sweetness burned.

The man made us a curly kind of green pasta. I coughed when I tried to eat it, took the noodles out of my mouth and put them on the table.

"Milly, don't be like that," Mom said. She had a dark dry line of purple across her lower lip.

"It's too spicy for her, is all," the man said. "Here, let me rinse them," and he put my noodles in a colander and ran cold water over them, then poured them back into my bowl. They didn't taste like anything then, except water, which was how I liked them.

Mom swirled wine in her glass. She wore earrings that stretched her earlobes.

"OK, Scoobers," she said. "You must be wiped out. Time for bed."

"I'm not wiped out," I said.

"We all are. Do you want to stay up alone?"

I shook my head. She and the man took me into a room with lots of windows covered in bars. There was a pullout couch.

"Don't I have to brush my teeth?"

"Not tonight," Mom said. She talked too close to my face. Her face was big and flushed and beautiful.

"I'm not calling," I heard her yell through the wall. "So just tell me to leave."

"You *will* stay, but I would like for you to call. He would like to know you two are safe."

"He knows I'm not safe," she said.

Mom's voice was higher and slower than normal. It didn't sound like her. I got up to check that it was still her. The light was off in the kitchen but there were candles. Her blue kimono was on the ground. She leaned against the re-frigerator, knocking off magnets.

"I used to be really good," she said, and he said, "Shhh shhh shhh, come on. Have some water." She swayed.

"I'm fucking it all up. What's safe about that?"

"Easy, my love. We're all right."

She hung her head. The wig slipped to the floor.

"Tell me," she said, "wasn't I a good dancer?"

He held a cup of water to her mouth but she swung her head away.

"I tried so hard," she said.

"I know. Let's go to bed."

"Mom?" I said from the doorway.

"Oh God, get her out of here," she said.

Back in bed I hugged the doll's hard body and wished for a Glow Baby, her body lit red like when I pressed a flashlight's beam to the inside of my cheek. Across the room was a desk with a black, gooseneck lamp. I brought my doll to the desk, clicked on the lamp, and held her head to the light bulb. She glowed a soft red to her fingertips, just like a Glow Baby. I touched her cheek. She grew warm, and her hair began to smoke. Her face folded in on itself. I must have called for

Mom. The man broke in, a sheet around his waist. He grabbed the flaming doll from my hands and tossed her into a metal garbage can.

"I'm here," Mom said. She took me in her arms, rocked me on the bed. "We're OK, we're OK, we're OK."

"Take her out of the garbage," I said.

"She doesn't look so well," he said, but Mom reached for her. I couldn't look at the doll again. I made him wrap her in a white dishcloth and hide the bundle between socks in his top dresser drawer.

"I'm sleeping with Milly," Mom told the man. He left, the sheet trailing behind him.

She pinched at the burned place on my robe's sleeve.

"Scoob," she said. She was crying. I stroked the inside of her wrist with one finger.

"I don't know how I could say that, about not being your mom. Of course I am. Don't let me say anything like that again."

I nodded. I traced the veins up her arm as far as they went.

"I'll always be your mom."

"You will," I said.

I wondered about the doll's face, wrapped up in the white cloth.

"Tell me a story," I said.

She told me about her dance. It began in darkness and silence; no one wanted to breathe. And then a bird started singing in the darkness, which was sort of like a kind of light, she said. Then another bird started to sing, and another, and the lights came up as the birdsong grew louder. She danced like the birds were singing inside her, hoping to get out. It was like a whole forest trapped in her, she said. It was the sound of the sun rising.

"What were you wearing?" I said.

"Look, it's my dance I'm trying to tell you about."

"You did."

"I was wearing a white dress. Listen," she said, "I think that's rain."

She grabbed my hand and led me through the kitchen into the storm.

In the morning I woke up in bed next to Mom, clinging to her and shivering, mud caked on my legs. It felt good to scratch it. By the time Dad arrived, I had a fever of 103, and Mom screamed at the man for calling Dad and screamed at Dad for coming but let him pull us both in and hold us, heat radiant around me, the kitchen surrounding us smudged and bright, My girls, he said, what did you do, my girls. And when he took her home, her hair grew back threaded with gray, and she kept it cropped at her chin. She lost and then gained a great deal of weight, and Dad sold her red car, and we moved to a different house, inland, with lower taxes and no fields or beaches. For a time she paced up and down the driveway, and then stopped leaving the house altogether, and pulled a plastic lawn chair into the shower because she felt too weak to stand in the steam. When a bird flew in through the kitchen window and battered back and forth against the walls she locked herself in her bedroom for three days. I never found its body.

But the night of the storm Mom whooped in the cold, and I chased her through the darkness across the slippery lawn, my feet slithering in the mud.

"Listen to it," she shouted, "Let yourself dance," and her white shape writhed and spun and I let my arms go and threw myself down on the ground, rolling and tossing my head. I listened as hard as I could, and tried not to scream, though I could feel something waking up inside me, wanting to come out, so I chased Mom's shape through the dark, and I danced the scream instead.

Goodnight, Beautiful Women

Mom paces the living room, head down, arms to her sides, fingers curled in loose fists. Her mouth hangs open. This is her concentration face. She used to make it fingerpicking her guitar or changing lanes.

"How doin', baby?" Bert says. I kiss her cheek at bedtime, slowing her.

She moves tentatively, like a blind woman whose furniture has been rearranged, trying to carve away the strangeness of new space. I fall asleep to her footsteps and wake in the night to creaking floorboards, the sound of her shuffling. I should be worried, I am, but it's comforting too—ice caked against my windowsill, our two longhaired cats, mother and daughter, flanking me on both sides, the midnight routine of Bert stoking the woodstove, and her footsteps. I count them.

She walks the same course. A tight circle around the lamp, the length of the bookshelf, seven steps, the length of the fireplace, five.

In the morning I block her way and hug her. Her head tucks easily beneath my chin. She seems smaller all the time, but I am too tall, still growing, looming over her like the boys I dance with. We spin in a slow circle.

"If you had any idea how much we miss you," she says. "Some days I'm so mad at your dad for paying your way out of here, even though it's the one good thing he's done. I know you're better off studying, not growing up to live in a trailer in the front yard. But the horrible thing is I would rejoice to have you in that trailer." She pulls away and shakes her hands like she's drying them.

"Forget that," she says. I wipe under her eyes with my thumb. The skin there is papery, dark as a bruised fruit. "I've got to get out of this house. This town, too. It's just too fucking cold."

For the past few years, since I've been in boarding school, she hasn't gotten in a car except to drive to her appointments. Bert's the one who does the grocery shopping. When she wants a vegetable he brings home frozen blocks of peas and goopy Vidalia onions. Last time Mom and I went on a trip I was in the fourth grade. We left Bert behind. My teacher made me keep a journal since Mom took me away during school. We drove to Vermont, so I filled the journal's pages by gluing on dead leaves.

"Plus Bert's never left Maine," Mom says. "You can't just never leave a place."

Bert's down on the floor, wrestling a strand of partially-swallowed tinsel from the cat's mouth.

"Once they start swallowing it they just can't stop," he tells us.

"Tuscany," Mom says. "Florida. Someplace sandy, maybe."

"Kerguelen!" says Bert.

"No more," Mom says. She lights a joint. "He's obsessed."

"Called Desolation Island," he says, starting the burner under Jimmy Dean with tater tots, his specialty breakfast. "Fifty French scientists, three thousand miles from land. They eat cabbages and sheep. The island is crawling with feral cats."

"We already live on desolation island," Mom says. She's throwing clothes from their hangers onto the bed.

"What can I do ya for, honey?" Bert yells.

"Will you tell him I don't want anything?" she says to me, and I lean into the kitchen and tell him, "Make her an egg," so he can say back, "Poof, she's an egg," and he does.

In the bedroom Mom's standing in front of the mirror in her red cowboy boots. They're crumpled, streaked with dust. She wore them for months after she left Dad. She wore them out dancing, brought men home in them. For a while before Bert, Mom and I lived in an Airstream by a rock quarry. Late at night I could hear the boot's heels clicking sharply against the quarry's pink granite.

She's wearing the same clothes as the day before, her sweater slipping off one shoulder. "Well, would you look at her," she says, stooping to spit shine the leather.

We take the white 1989 Volvo. Bert says it handles the road best of all our shit-box cars, even though the muffler's on its way out and the horn's busted. He keeps an air horn in the cup holder in case of emergencies.

On the way to the car Bert reaches into the garden's winter tangle of weeds to rub the head of our Saint Francis statue for luck, but he's the wrong saint. Saint Christopher is the patron saint of travel, and Saint Francis is the patron saint of animals.

We drive past the church and the library closed for winter, the gray harbor stripped of boats, and the mottled docks hauled up on the beach. The few remaining buoys bob on the choppy water.

I press my forehead to the cool window and let my shoulders drop with relief that I'm leaving. Going home is a terrible feeling. It's like film moving backward, a butterfly's blood sucked back to the center of its body with a swift collapse of wings, the return to the chrysalis. It makes me feel sick.

When I think of home I think of Mom where I usually find her, buried under blankets, cold cups of coffee leaving rings on her bedside table. I think of the doctor, who warned her at her last physical that her muscles are starting to atrophy. I've got to spend my life moving out, until that day when Bert's artery clogs, or Mom finds a lump, and I move back in. But now she's got her red boots propped up on the dashboard, and she's singing along to the radio, and we're squealing out onto Route 1.

By the time we cross the bridge out of state I'm up front and Mom's crawled into the backseat to shut her eyes. She hugs an old sock monkey of mine. "I made it," Bert says, thumping the broken horn in reflexive celebration. We cruise over the bridge at seventy, our tires singing on the grated iron.

"What do you say that is?" he asks me. "That little light, moving strange?" It's four thirty, but the sun's gone down and the moon is lost in cloud cover. The windows of homes across the bay are blinking on, yellow and small. A bright-blue dot bobs over the horizon.

"Sailboat mast."

"Right again," Bert says. "Thought I'd found a UFO." He looks at me as he drives, weaving along the slushy center lane, talking theories about the end of the Mayan calendar. How aliens probably won't come, but something bad will. The snow hisses under our wheels. Eyes flash from the ditches. Mom's teeth make a stony sound as she grinds them in her sleep. Bert's saying something about the sun's orbit being like a carousel horse, going up and down as it circles the galaxy. And then he's talking about the magnetic poles flipping, birds flying in the wrong direction, looting and mayhem, but I'm still thinking about a carousel horse, its teeth bared around the bit.

At the gas station we buy her presents. Bert picks the wrong things—Jujubee candies and Cadbury eggs with marshmallow cream centers—and I pick the right ones—salt and vinegar chips and bars of dark chocolate that she nibbles one square at a time.

"Ick," she says of the Jujubees, shaking them into her hands. "But I do think they're beautiful. When I was little, I wanted to change my name to Jujubee. I begged for it."

"It's not too late," Bert says. He scoops the candies from her palm, throws the whole handful into his mouth. Melted color is left behind where she held them.

She gets out to stretch, staggers. Bert loops his arm around her waist, holding the belt buckle of her jeans.

"The boots?" I say.

"Meds. Throw off my inner ear." She clicks the boots together like ruby slippers.

A pack of blondes tumbles from a green van, glancing at us.

"Yep," Bert says. "We're in the real world. Time for a haircut and a beard trim."

He's eating a Little Debbie apple pie, and Mom digs the wad of Kleenex from her pocket, cleans his beard of jelly. Since I was last home his wild beard has gone gray.

"I can't be trusted anymore," she says. "You should have seen the latest hack job I gave him. He won't let anyone but me cut it. Except you, maybe."

"Only you," he says to her, tucking his hand into the back pocket of her jeans.

"People will think we're gypsies," she says.

* * *

128

Bert does all the driving. I didn't get my learner's permit because he liked to drive me so much. He's been with Mom for ten years, and spent a lot of that time taking me to town and back in his truck. It was the only time he would really talk. I'd get him going on the easy stuff, like the planets and their moons, or Nostradamus, or the reptilian elite. Then he'd say something about Mom, how he'd been trying to cook something that would make her want to eat. How he didn't know what to do to cheer her up. Bert trying to cheer up Mom usually involves him walking into her bedroom and flashing her his stomach, fast, like a toddler. And all I'd say would be "I know." And then I'd say one of my worries about Mom and all he'd say would be "I know." Back and forth like that.

The motel room smells like feet and chemicals. Bert puts on the coffee. I arrange the soaps into the shape of a fan inside their wicker basket. Mom lays sheets of newspaper over the carpet. Outside, rain darkens the parking lot. Bert switches the TV channel to a show on female bodybuilders. He cranks up the volume, drowning out the gurgling coffee machine and the huffing heater installed between the beds. Mom takes his head in her hands.

"You see what I live with?" she says to me. "Just the two of us? It's inescapable."

"Maybe what you guys need is a foster child," I say.

She snips at his long hair and beard, the fine gray-blond clippings falling at her feet. Her big toe is bruised under the nail. She starts to cry, soundlessly.

"Well, that hurt," Mom says softly to Bert. There is a round of rowdy applause from the studio audience.

"Yep," Bert says.

"I never thought of that one. Just adopt a new child. Easy."

It sounds different coming out of her mouth.

"I'm right here," I say. "I only meant because you're good parents."

"I know what you meant," she says, stepping back to eye Bert. He flexes, running a hand through his hair, which sticks out around his ears. I can see the scissor marks. His beard is shorter on one side than the other. They move close, crunching the newspaper.

"You look like you've escaped the nut house," she says.

Mom has been paying for this trip with Bert's birthday gift, one hundred Sacagawea coins, double the years of her life. She keeps the coins in a purple satchel, and takes her time doling them out, dropping them one by one into the palm of the drive-thru cashier, or the red-faced woman who pumps our gas. When we leave our Motel 6 room covered in hair and newspaper, Bert's sweet-smelling tobacco ground into the rug, Mom tips the maid with the last of her gold. She lingers by the nightstand, touching the coin like a magpie with a shiny wrapper.

We go off route. Bert hands me the map, but I can't get oriented. He speeds over hills, our stomachs cresting and plummeting. We take the blue highways through West Virginia and Kentucky, waiting for willow trees and cicadas and a warm breeze. The towns we pass look like home – trailers with scabby patches of yellow grass, kids' plastic trikes, and broken trampolines. People glare from their porches, white breath hanging in the air from cigarettes or cold. We crack the windows and shiver.

Mom holds the air horn in front of her like a weapon, ready to blare at offending cars. Bert fiddles with the radio dial as he drives and lands on the news—talk of swine flu and next summer's storms. Hurricane Wilma is mentioned and after that he won't stop bellowing "Willllllllllmaaaaa!" like Fred Flintstone.

"If the flu hits, God help me you are coming home," Mom says. I laugh.

"You think I'm kidding? We've already stocked up on canned goods. Nothing funny about a pandemic."

"And I'll shoot anyone with the crossbow who tries to break in and eat our food," Bert says, working a red Swedish Fish around in his mouth.

She twists to face me, and grips my knee.

"I don't think you understand," she says, her lips barely moving. "I'm talking about the black plague here. I'm talking about sores all over your body, and the young dying first, in a matter of days. Projectile vomit. Please, if you let me do one thing for you, let me fear your death." She leans back in her seat and takes a sip of water, which spills as we round a bend.

"Wet T-shirt contest," Bert says.

The light lasts longer. "It's warm enough that there's color," Mom says. We drive until we find a field, anyone's field, and pull the car over to sleep. The field is dusky hay, wild around the car but stretching off into trampled-looking furrows. I curl up in the way back and Bert and Mom recline their seats. Bert gives me his winter coat for extra warmth. I pop the collar. The coat holds his smell—brushfires and pot smoke and pine.

"Compared to Motel 6, this Volvo is like the Ritz," he says. They can see the stars through the sunroof. He knows the names of the constellations, and he lists them for us as we fall asleep. Capricornus, the sea goat. Mom laughs. Equuleus, the foal. Circinus, the compass. Andromeda, the chained lady.

"Goodnight, beautiful women," says Bert.

Hours later I wake up to what sounds like someone volleying a tennis ball back and forth before I realize it's just Bert's nose clicking as he snores. The sky is green through the back window. Mom is not in the car. She stands in the field, looking toward me, her figure blurred by the fogged glass.

I wonder if she is sleepwalking. I climb over the seat to roll down the car window. "What's wrong?" I whisper. She presses a many-ringed finger to her lips, gestures for me to join her. I wrap a blanket around my shoulders, quietly lift the latch. I'm barefoot, and the long grass is sharp and wet. I'm afraid I might step on a slug. She puts her arm around me. I'm shivering. A black cricket springs onto my foot and I shake it gone.

"I think I have to leave Bert," she says.

My mouth floods with spit. I hold my hand over my mouth, swallowing.

"I can't explain it," she says. Her voice is taut. I keep swallowing. "It's just the only thing I can do." She pulls her turtleneck up over her chin. "You have no idea how hard it is to live with someone who only reads the horoscope. Who says 'queechee' when he's ordering quiche. Who spends all his time thinking about these conspiracies. I'm waiting for the day I find him wearing a tin foil hat. That stuff is all he talks about. When he even talks to me. He doesn't, mostly. He talks to you." She takes my hand. "It feels like life or death."

Bert has known me since I was six. I remember the first time I saw him he was doing dishes. I stood on a stepstool next to him and put my hands in the hot dishwater. Later that day he taught me how to tie my shoes. Bert wears shoes that fasten with Velcro. When I come home on vacation he makes me beef stroganoff and molasses cookies. I am the only one who compliments his cooking, and he likes to joke with Mom that if they ever separated, I would go with him.

She hugs me, rocking us back and forth.

Before Mom met Bert he was drinking a fifth of Coffee Brandy a night and she was gearing up to get rune symbols tattooed around her waist like a belt. He met her at a party where she was flirting with everyone but him. He was lying on the couch, too drunk to stand, but by dawn he'd slept it off and was the only man fit to walk her home. He quit drinking the next day, and spent two winters building us a cabin.

I glance into the car. Bert is curled up in the seat. He's wearing an old T-shirt of mine that tells you about different kinds of whales.

We get back on the road before it's fully light out. Bert stops at a gas station to buy hot chocolates and Mom goes in with him. She comes back out alone. "I told him," she says, weeping, buckling into the driver's seat and starting the car. "I had to." She pulls out, tires squealing.

"We can't just go," I say.

"It's done. He doesn't want to go on with us."

I look back. Bert's standing outside the store, our two hot chocolates in his hands. His gray-blond hair is blowing like seeds from a kicked dandelion.

"Turn around," I say, but she won't.

I crank the window down and rest my cheek on the edge of the glass. I let the wind batter me. Each new moment as we speed away from Bert comes as a surprise: the trees blurring by, the white line steady on the road's shoulder.

I have felt this way before, when I was nine and my dog died. I went on a bicycle ride and suddenly couldn't believe I had the power to move my machine forward into each new, unfolding second. I kept waiting for the next second to be swallowed up in black. I guess I kept waiting to die.

Mom needs rest. She's so tired that the buildings going by are wavering a little, like heat shimmer above pavement.

"Say I'm drowning," she says. "I've been holding around Bert's neck for a long time. He's tired, too."

The motel smells the same as two nights ago, and the soaps are the same, the very same brand, and I feel like I'm in a dream. Mom crawls into bed and I don't know what to do for her. I run a bath. And here I am in the bath, swishing my hair back and forth, watching the water drain. And here are my hands, pulling a blanket up over her. She is asleep. She flutters her eyes open once when I get into bed beside her but I don't think she's seeing me. When I lean in, I can feel the heat radiating off her, tiny suns tucked around her body. And here I am kissing her forehead. She tastes like salt.

Driving isn't so hard. There's a rock caught in the front tire, and as I accelerate the *tick tick tick* grows faster and that's all I'm listening to. I park crooked at the gas station and run in, a bell sounding. Past the flurry machine, the red hotdogs steaming in their case, the motor oil, and the sunglasses stand. Bert's not there. I knock on the door to the men's room, open it. It's empty. I was positive this was the same gas station, but now I'm not so sure.

I run back to the parking lot and grab the air horn. Start honking it. It's louder than I imagined it would be. No one's at the pump, but the cashier comes to the window. I keep blaring the horn. A line of crows scatters from the telephone wire. After fifteen honks it runs out of air, hissing. The cashier shouts at me from the doorway, but I can't hear what she's saying. When my ears stop ringing, she's still waiting there, looking at me, her hands on her hips as though I'm supposed to say something. I climb into the front seat of the car. She watches me. I dig Bert's orange cap out from under the front seat and pull it on. I wait for him to come back, but he doesn't.

By the time I'm driving ninety toward the horizon, sunroof open and windows down, the car doesn't smell like Bert anymore.

Werewolf

Already, what a day. Claire can't open her eyes because of what she might see—their clothes scattered on the floor, the glass of orange juice and water on the bedside table with the pulp settled to a cloud at the bottom, and her lipstick blotting its rim, accusatory somehow, as the glasses she unloads from the dishwasher, clean save for her stubborn lipstick, are also accusatory. She has to put them through the dishwasher twice. In the kitchen now is a stack of dirty dishes. When she and Hal returned from last night's party she plunged her arm into the greasy gray dishwater to scoop the drain free of food. She had walked the oatmeal slop to the bathroom to blame him. "This is truly disgusting," she said. "This is what happens when you don't scrape them." But it was her fault, too, for making oatmeal every morning and leaving the dirty pot on the stove.

ANNA NOYES

Then they fought in the shower because she had wanted
to leave the party earlier than he did. They were both drunk,
and Hal stood under the stream of hot water with his eyes
closed and his hair plastered to his forehead while she talked
at him. When she started to sob, Hal hugged her, and the
water streamed between their stomachs. She knew that by
crying she had won Hal's tenderness.

There was a cold entity inside her that rose out and
watched. *Werewolf*, she thought, and this disturbed her. She
rarely acknowledged this second self. In the past, when
she became aware of it, her private thought was that this
witness self was something that brought her closer to God.
She had never thought of it as malicious. *Werewolf*. The
water ran too hot, and her stomach turned. She thought,
what if I am bad?

Before bed she climbed on top of Hal and had sex the
way she did when she was drunk. To fall asleep she said a
mantra to herself so she would stop thinking about badness
or goodness.

The next morning Hal's arm is slung over her body.
Some drama peaks in his dream and his hand spasms, squeezing the little pouch her stomach makes when she lies on her
side. It startles her. The sudden awareness of her stomach
makes her queasy. Though she shouldn't feel that way. It is
a good body.

It's hangovers that make her body feel most uninhabitable
—physically with nausea, but also, perhaps primarily, because
she is wracked with guilt. She is married, she has her own

138

family unit now, and soon, maybe in a year or so, she hopes to have a baby. Still, the morning after she drinks, her mind goes right to her parents, as though she's let them down. It makes no sense.

She wants to sleep all day, but today is her Sunday with Paul. By now he has probably showered, dressed, and put on his cologne, and is waiting outside for her, as he does even on the coldest days, even when she calls to tell his aide she's running late. Or once, when she had to cancel, the aide couldn't get him to come back inside. Not for a couple hours.

She gets out of bed, knowing she can bear it. Even Paul's cologne (her own doing, a present from the discount bin) that he douses himself with is something she will bear.

Today needs a lot of makeup, and she takes her time bringing her face back to life. Her eyes are rimmed red from the crying. Hal comes into the bathroom and runs his nails across her bare back. "That was some hot lovemaking," he says. Their lovemaking, like her crying, is slightly hazy. But she knows she was somehow better. As in, wilder. He wraps his arms around her and puts his mouth to her ear, "My werewolf."

The sudden clarity of that word, breathed against her ear, jolts her. It was like gunpoint, which is crazy, but that was her thought—*a gun*.

It's like he's found her out.

"Don't call me that," she says.

"You're pretty proud of yourself aren't you? Fooling everyone."

"Am not," says Claire. "I really don't understand the rules. I hate that game. I hate being werewolf. It makes me so nervous." She does, she hates the game.

He runs his hands over her hip bones.

"Hello, it's me," he says. "I'm your husband, remember? You can't fool me. I see you. You're playing the game right now."

"Please," she says, and can feel her palms and feet begin to sweat. "I really don't. I don't get it."

"Come on, now. Drop the fake-innocence shtick. There's no one watching."

"Give me a break," she says, applying her lipstick. She draws her lips in neatly and turns around to kiss Hal. His beard is wet, and he tastes of mint and last night's drinks. He tries to dart his tongue into her mouth, but she pulls away and burrows her face into the warm darkness of his neck.

Hal knows her, and of course he is right. She's still playing.

But I really don't *know how the game is played,* she thinks. *And it really* does *make me nervous.*

And who is defensive in this way? It is the werewolf. She thought it was Claire for a moment, but it was still the werewolf.

Last night, when the party was winding down the group gathered to play Werewolf. She announced to Hal, just loud enough for the circle of players to hear, that she was scared to death of being chosen as werewolf. That whoever was God, who did the choosing, better not pick her. She was naïve;

she was nervous. But the werewolf was conniving. Through announcing her fear, she ensured she would be chosen as werewolf, and that the others would not suspect nervous, sweet Claire. Already the werewolf was strategizing. But Claire was separate from that. Claire was afraid.

In the beginning, she really didn't understand just how the game was played. At least, certain minor components, like the detective or the guardian angel. But what she did understand was her own role as werewolf, in which everyone would close their eyes and pretend to be a town that had gone to sleep, and then God, played by one of her friends, would tell the werewolf to open their eyes and "kill" someone. At this point she felt her face change from its peaceful, sleeping state to something maniacal and feral, and she'd open her eyes and point to the person she wanted to kill, careful not to rustle her dress as she pointed. Then she'd return her face to its sleeping peacefulness so she could wake authentically as a townsperson and talk over who they all suspected the werewolf to be.

After each killing, Claire tried to be kind—defensive of those who were accused of being the werewolf and suspicious only of those making accusations. And throughout each round Claire asked questions about how the game was played, answers, in all honesty, she did not have figured out.

She reapplies her lipstick, which is smudged from kissing Hal.

It was effortless to play the part of a townsperson. She just played herself. All she had to do was shut off the part

141

of her brain that knew she was the werewolf. In that way it didn't feel like lying. Between killings she thought nothing of the werewolf.

At the end of the game, once everyone had been killed off with no votes accusing her, she revealed her identity. Her friends shook their heads in disbelief and laughter, and glanced sidelong at her, saying things like, "You think you know someone."

Because she couldn't deceive her closest friend at the party, or Hal, she killed them off in the first and second rounds so she wouldn't have to.

She says to Hal, "You're right. I'm a mastermind, and I'm playing the game right now." It comes out sarcastic when she means it to sound genuine, a confession to uproot the werewolf's strategy.

How absurd, to be thinking *mastermind* about a silly game that necessitates manipulation and deceit. That's just how you play if you want to win.

But it's not the game, she thinks, in the car to pick up Paul with the radio blasting for distraction. It's what the game reveals: that all the sweetness and kindness and feelings and tears that she displays to the world could be driven by some essentially bad second self.

She isn't sure what that second self wants, but it has something to do with winning.

As a child, she was a liar.

The first lie she remembers, she was waiting for the school bus with her dad in his truck. It was raining. The bus sped past their driveway without stopping, so her dad honked the horn and the bus pulled over. She had to get out and run through the rain. When she boarded, a bully who was in her first-grade class said, "Hey, isn't it your *birthday*?" The bus lurched forward, and Claire nodded yes even though her birthday was the next day, and braced herself down the aisle of seats. The bus driver overheard and he made the bus sing while Claire stared out the window. At school they announced the lie over the intercom, her class sang also, and her teacher gave her a cupcake with a candle in it. "But your birthday's tomorrow," her friend said as she was blowing out the candle. "No it isn't," said Claire. "Then why is your party tomorrow?" She couldn't swallow the cupcake, so she wrapped it in a paper napkin and crushed it into her pocket. "It's not," she said. "It's canceled."

She sobbed as soon as she came home and saw her dad. While she confessed he held her in his lap, even though her rain gear was dripping wet. The next day, her real birthday, passed like any other regular day.

The second, playing Marco Polo on the playground, she sprinted with her eyes closed into the slide. Her mouth was bleeding, and she ran her tongue over the jagged stub where her front tooth had been, a tooth that had grown in the month before. When she opened her mouth, her friends gaped and said, "Oh my God," some screaming and some laughing.

When her parents came to pick her up, she told them that someone had pushed her into the slide. They wanted the bully's name. In Claire's teens, when her fake tooth still gave her problems (a root canal, bloody gums), her dad said, "Come on, out with it, stop protecting that little fucker." But she shook her head. She couldn't confess. Too much time had gone by.

And then there was the third.

She was sitting on the pink window seat at her grandma's house. It must have been Christmas, because Paul, her cousin, and his little brother, Reuben, were there with their mom, Aunt Ray. Claire was six at the time, which would've made Reuben seven and Paul nine. She can even remember her shirt: plaid and red. Her mom knew something was wrong, even before Claire left dinner and went to the window seat to be alone. Her mom followed.

Here's what she didn't want to tell: earlier that day, a man who worked on her grandmother's farm took her into an old gardening shed that had been converted into a playhouse for the children. There were bunk beds inside the playhouse. They climbed up to the top bunk. The man took his pants off and asked her to touch him. She doesn't remember if she did or not. All she remembers is that he kissed her, deeply enough so that she could feel that he had no teeth. She wanted to get away, but was afraid of going down ladders.

So instead she told her mom that she'd been playing with her cousins in the bath that day, and Paul went outside and came back with a stick and poked her with it.

Her cousins were upstairs getting ready for bed, and her mom took her hand and led her to the bottom of the stairwell, and yelled up for them, her voice shaking in fear and anger. Paul and Reuben came and stood on the stairs, in the Christmas hats that Grandma had knit for all three kids, lumpy hats with bells and too many points.

"Paul," said Claire's mom, "did you poke Claire with a stick?" "What?" asked Paul. And her mom said, "So you didn't go get a stick while Claire was in the bath and poke her with it?" Paul shook his head. Reuben shook his head also and said, "We didn't even have a bath today." Then Aunt Ray came to the top of the stairs and Claire's mom explained again what had happened. Ray went down to where Paul was standing on the stairwell in his Christmas hat, his cheeks red as he started to cry. She put her arms over his shoulders and asked, "Did you hurt Claire in the bath?" And Paul said, "No," and Reuben said, "I swear it, he didn't."

Reuben was always defending Paul, because Paul had Down syndrome and was smaller than Reuben, though he was two years older. It went like that for a long time, her cousins, who were her best friends, looking down at her in bewilderment and her aunt with her arms over Paul's shoulders, saying, "But it's true, I gave them their bath last night. They didn't take a bath today."

Why Claire told this lie she doesn't understand. She said Paul had poked her, but she doesn't remember specifying that he poked her between the legs, though she must have said so. And she remembers the lies she told in the doctor's office later that week so vividly, as though the resolution of her life was turned up for that one moment, but turned down again for the part where he examined her, which she doesn't remember at all. She remembers sitting on the edge of the exam table in her paper gown, searching her imagination for details to make the lie richer—Paul went outside (here she imagined him going out the back door) and found a stick in the snow (she imagined him searching by their grandma's hedge) and brought it back inside. "It still had some snow on it," she told the doctor.

Years later her mom would remark on the calmness and clarity with which Claire was able to express what had happened to her. And at only six years old. Her mom recounted the story many times, but only to Claire. How brave Claire was for such a little kid, and how her mom had known, had just known, that something wasn't right. Her mom used the word "abuse" for what had happened with the stick in the bathtub. Though of course it was complicated, since Paul was also so little, since he had Down syndrome.

Why Paul? She could just as easily have accused Reuben. Or was it possible that even at age six she knew that Paul was the weaker one, that people would only believe the lie if it were her word against his?

Afterward, when Aunt Ray folded Claire into hugs, the soft of her body and strong arms and wool sweater warm and comforting, she'd pull back and fix Claire with a knowing look that said, *They think you're so sweet but I see you.* At family dinners she'd draw her son into her lap and stroke Paul's hair and cheeks and let him eat with his fingers off her dinner plate, and she'd watch Claire. Or so it seemed. Claire—with her good grades, dance recitals, and plays all through middle school and then high school, while Reuben stole candy, then lighters, then beer, and Paul got fat. Paul ate and ate and ate at these family dinners, heaping his plate with spaghetti and garlic bread; and though as a little boy he was so thin his skin was almost translucent, he grew into a two-hundred-pound, five-foot-tall teenager. One summer night their grandma had yelled at him across the dinner table, "Stop jamming your face," and said to Ray, "Your boy's a pig. Why don't you teach him manners?"

"You're all a bunch of assholes," Ray said. She pushed her chair back and it fell over. She went out on the porch, slamming the door so hard behind her that it bounced back open and stayed that way, as Ray's cigarette smoke drifted into the kitchen.

"Oh that's good, swear in front of the kids," Grandma yelled out to her. "No wonder your boys are such animals."

Paul continued eating his spaghetti, neatly dabbing his mouth with a napkin after each bite. Claire began to clear the table. "Good girl," her grandma said.

And throughout boarding school and college and afterward, when she brought home clean-cut boyfriends and then married one of them, she was a good girl. She picked up Paul from his group home every Sunday. They went to the Y and floated around and then they went to Denny's for dinner, or sometimes the sub-sandwich place, and afterward a movie at the theater or else she bought him VHS tapes for a dollar apiece at the Goodwill. She never watched those tapes with him though—she'd only once visited his group home, a trailer that smelled of overcooked batches of hamburger meat that the aide cooked up for nightly dinners. The aide, a slouchy, nearly humpbacked woman on oxygen named Pam, had them all join hands while she recited the Lord's Prayer. After Pam prayed, Paul said he would like to say a prayer also, and he put his hands together in front of his heart and said that the Lord had made this his family, and would He please protect them all, and then, with his eyes squeezed shut, he said he could hear Grandma saying from heaven that she loved everyone and that Claire was an angel, amen. Claire forced the gray meat into her mouth and drank the glass of water full of ice cubes that tasted like freezer.

After dinner Claire sat on Paul's bed and watched one of the VHS tapes she'd bought him. It was called *Air Bud*, about a golden retriever that played basketball. His room smelled of mildew and grape air freshener, and there were two towels tacked over the only window. An air-conditioning unit was on, and the air made the towels flutter out into the room.

After that first and only visit, she kept Paul out for longer and took him to the nighttime movies sometimes, which cost five dollars more than the matinees. She let him get whatever he wanted at Denny's, though she knew it was wrong to let him eat like that (double bacon cheeseburgers with ketchup and extra pickles, but no onion, mustard, lettuce, or tomato) with his weak heart and all. That people with Down syndrome died early was a thing she knew but didn't understand, had never looked into enough to understand; she couldn't look into it, could hardly think about it. She had never seen a person with Down syndrome who had gray hair or wrinkles, but then again she hadn't seen many others with Down syndrome, only a memorable few, perhaps a dozen.

In the back of her mind, Hal's voice is looping, *You're playing right now*, and the wheel grows sticky beneath her palms. *Right now. And now.*

When Claire was seventeen, Aunt Ray got sick, and she knew she had to confess. But first she confessed to her mother.

Most of all it troubled her how she'd let her mom tell and retell and retell the story of the lie to herself and to Claire, as an exemplary triumph of motherly intuition, and of Claire's maturity in being so clear and so honest.

The brain is a tricky place, and in certain moods Claire trusted the confusion that followed her confession.

"But just a second," said her mom, after Claire told her about the man on the bunk bed ("Oh, honey," she'd said, and started to cry) and confessed that she had made up the whole story about Paul. "You say you were upset about the man, whatever happened with the man, but the stuff with Paul happened over Christmas. Your grandma didn't have hired help at Christmas. That must have been the summer, when the man did that to you."

But the unreliable time line didn't seem like the point. Claire could have simply been *thinking* about the man, perhaps what happened with him had happened on a different day, months earlier, but was on her mind when her mom cornered her on the window seat. Claire's head was in her mom's lap, and her mom was petting her hair. "You poor thing," she said. "This kills me. You were so little. Little kids don't deserve this kind of shit."

"But see, I know the whole thing with Paul was a lie," Claire said. "I'm certain. I can remember, so distinctly, how it felt to tell the lies. At the doctor's. Making up that stuff about the snow. All of it."

"What else do you remember?"

"Not much else," she said. She didn't. Everything around the lies was blurry.

Her mother recalled how after she confessed what Paul had done to her, when she went pee she would scream and scream. "It stings," she would scream, "it *stings*." When the doctor examined her, he had found small cuts on her labia. But he would not look inside her; he thought it would be too painful. He thought perhaps a piece of the stick was still inside, but said he would let it come out on its own.

Her mom patted her hair, and Claire cried into her lap, as they talked about the strangeness of memory, and how ashamed she must have felt, with her aunt and her cousins looking down at her from the stairwell, denying her story.

"But it's true," Claire said, "we hadn't had a bath that day. I know we didn't have a bath."

"You're right. Not with *water*. You were in the tub though, playing naked. That's what you told the doctor."

"I don't remember."

"I'm amazed you remember any of it," her mom said, kissing Claire's hair. "You were a tiny doobie. And everything turned out OK. Why don't you give that little girl a break?"

Claire thought about herself as a little girl, standing at the bottom of the stairwell, and wanted to soften to the image. But what she saw was a six-year-old too tall and too smart for her own good, easily repeating the narrative of her lie, caught up in the course of it, too cowardly to unravel it.

"Aunt Ray knows," Claire said. "That's why she hates me. I know you don't see it, but I do. She looks at me funny."

"Oh, Ray's just a bitch. Excuse me, I love her, she's sick, but she's also one of the best bitches around. So cut her some slack. Cut yourself some. Don't be so hard on yourself all the time," her mom said. "That kind of shit will hurt you."

And the part of herself that invests in being a good daughter, wife, and friend, the part that she grooms every day and puts lipstick on, the part that takes Paul to dinner and screams, "Swim like hell, Paul!" at the Special Olympics, believes that through a trick of memory she deceived herself all these years into thinking she told a lie when really she never lied at all.

Yet in a cold, reserved place, a dark, blue-colored place somewhere beneath her heart, is the solid certainty that the doctor got something wrong. In this place, which is something like a cave, she is *certain*—she has no doubts whatsoever—that she lied.

When she pulls into the driveway of the group home, Paul is sitting on a boulder on the lawn, dressed all in red, cross-legged and huge like the laughing Buddha.

"Hello there, beautiful," he says, which he pronounces *bootiful*, a word Claire sometimes parrots to Hal ("Good morning, *bootiful*") without thinking about it.

"You're beautiful," she replies.

He runs his hand through his hair. "I know it."

"What's with the red? It's striking." For years he's worn monochromatic outfits, alternating white or black, but the red is new. She bought him these red pants, she recognizes, along with a white-and-black pair, in the women's plus-size leisure section at Walmart.

"I'm the Red Avenger," Paul says.

She laughs. "Who do you avenge?"

"Oh you know, bad guys, Doctor Doom, Riddler, that sort of thing." He lists a number of other villains from movies she doesn't recognize.

"So, baby," he says, pretend yawning and stretching so that he can throw one arm around her shoulder as she drives. "How about, for our date, there's this great Italian restaurant I know of."

"Oh yeah? Here in town?" He's squeezing her arm, leaning close to her face.

"OK, OK, stud," she says, "breathing room . . ." He draws his arm away and says, "OK, OK, jeez. I can take a hint," but he is smiling, joking. This is part of their routine.

"They have new pasta specials there, really nice pastas, and salads. It's called Pizza Hut. Have you ever ate there?"

"Let's do it," Claire says.

Settling in across the booth from him, she sees he is wearing a headset, what looks like a Bluetooth ear piece.

"Sweet phone," she says. "Who do you talk to?"

"Lots of people," he says, shrugging. "My brother in Rhode Island sometimes, you know, it was my brother's birthday so I called him the other night. And my darling cousin," he gestures largely at Claire across the table, "and sometimes, you know, I talk to my mom, Pamela, stuff like that."

"You talk to your mom?"

"Yeah, I talk to my mom, Pamela, you know, my friends."

"What does your mom say?"

"That you and I are going to get married."

"I miss her." Claire does not really miss her. There are a few moments that she misses. Like when Aunt Ray drove into town every summer in her Chinook RV. There were two narrow beds and a hot plate in the back. Ray would take them to the lake, and afterward they'd play house in the Chinook, getting sand between the sheets. And after the lake, that sand was gritty on Claire's scalp for hours. She'd lie in bed scratching her head, her fingernails dark with sand. But that was more about missing her childhood than it was about missing Ray.

"Don't you miss her?" Claire says.

"Well, sort of. I mean, I talk to her whenever I want." He shrugs again and closes his eyes, adjusting the headset so his mouth aligns with the microphone. "Mom?" he says. "It's Paul. Are you there?"

But then the doors to the kitchen swing open, and the pizza is coming toward them. He opens his eyes and says, "Sometimes she's not there."

If Claire were playing against Aunt Ray in Werewolf, Claire wouldn't kill her, though her aunt would be her biggest threat because she was the only person who was convinced that Claire was deceitful. It made your motivations obvious, if you killed off your enemies too soon.

But life wasn't like Werewolf, and Aunt Ray had died, at forty-six, of an ovarian tumor that spread throughout her body. Before she died she drove to Maine in the Chinook for the last time, settled Paul at the group home, and went to church with Claire and her mom, though none of them were year-round churchgoers under normal circumstances. Ray—who was almost six feet tall, and broad with a beautiful, stern face— had a glorious, full-throated wail of a voice that didn't fit with the quavering sopranos surrounding her, and she closed her eyes and stomped and swayed when she sang. Claire thought then maybe she wasn't the only one who felt small and weak next to Ray, chided simply by being in her presence.

In the hospital, Claire had feared Ray might finally call her out, but she didn't even look at her. Ray had each of her sons' hands on either shoulder, Claire's mom holding one foot and her grandma holding the other. Claire's hand didn't have a place, and so she rested it limply on her aunt's calf, against her bare skin, not sure if she should squeeze or pet her there. The leg seemed perfectly strong, as did her aunt's body beneath the hospital gown, but Ray's face had grown small and gaunt. Before she died she talked about cheeseburgers and Reuben's trombone playing and the new movies coming out and the dance that Paul was choreographing with the residents of his home. Then she stopped talking. She looked back and forth between her sons, taking in Reuben, then taking in Paul.

In the end Claire concluded that Ray didn't have the energy to bother with something so small as a false accusation over a stick. What was the consequence? Here were her teenage sons, flanking her, with their hands gripping her shoulders—Reuben's long, guitar-playing fingers and Paul's thick fingers, and the rings he liked to wear. They were almost grown-ups. Paul would have to keep on in the universe without his mom. They talked to her about everything—their lives, school, girls, all of it, even what they'd had for lunch that day. It was all vitally important. There was not one iota of spare space in Ray's heart to bother with the lie that had consumed Claire. And Claire saw that it didn't matter, lie or no lie—both were trivial. Trivial to Ray and to Paul, at least, and that was what mattered.

The summer after Ray died all the kids from town gathered at the river to play on the rope swing. Claire took Paul out of the group home for dinner at their grandma's, and after dinner she took him to the river. He was a good swimmer. All the summer kids were there—nameless batches of tan girls and boys who drove up from Connecticut to vacation for two weeks at a time, and the locals were there, too. They played a game called Crocodile Pit. You had to swing from one bank of the river to the other. When Paul took off his shirt, no one gawked, but she could sense their eyes on his belly, which sagged over the top of his swimming trunks. Everyone made it across the Crocodile Pit too quickly, within minutes it seemed, until there was only Paul and Claire alone on one side of the bank and the whole gang of kids on the other, watching and laughing and waiting. A boy swung the rope back to them.

"I got this," Paul said and cracked his knuckles. From across the bank, someone yelled, "Yeah, man."

"You sure?" Claire said. He nodded to her, "I'm sure," and gripped the rope. He leaped off and swung gracefully out over the river, everyone cheering and hooting, but his momentum wasn't strong enough to carry him all the way to the other side, or he was simply too heavy. He swung just inches short of the bank, and everyone let out a collective "Awww" as he swung back toward Claire, slower back and forth, until he hung clinging to the rope over the middle of the river.

"What do I do?" he shouted. The rope twisted him in one direction and then another.

"You'll be OK, just let go," Claire said.

"I'm too scared," Paul shouted. "I can't." He was crying loudly, and the kids at the other side had gone silent.

"Here, on three, just let your hands go, ready? One, two, three," said Claire. His swimming trunks were slipping down his hips, and his face turned red from the effort of holding on for so long. Still, she was surprised by his strength.

"I can't do it," he said. She watched as his hands lost their grip on the rope, inch by inch, and he yelped and cried. The rope spun him round and round until finally he fell into the water. He was screaming.

Paul resurfaced almost immediately. His body was always like that in water, effortlessly afloat. He could spend hours in the water when she took him to the pool, floating on his back like a pale, wide raft.

He crawled out on her side of the bank and pulled his trunks up. A boy from the other side of the river shouted across, "He's cool, right? We're going to go smoke," and with that, the group crunched off into the woods.

Paul sat cross-legged on a rock. He was crying. It got dark and chilly, and his clothes were wet, and he wouldn't talk to her. It was time to go. She took his hand and saw the red marks across his palms, slick and raw, from where the rope had burned him. They drove in silence, and she dropped him off like that, still crying, holding a tube of Neosporin. It was an unfair mess that Paul didn't have his mom anymore, and that he had to take his ointment and go inside and go to bed in a house full of strangers with his hands the way they were. But Claire was only seventeen then. She owed something to Ray, to Paul too, but she didn't know how to make good on it. So she started seeing him every Sunday. She'd only missed two Sundays in the past eleven years.

* * *

Paul has finished the pizza, all but the one slice Claire had taken for herself, which she picked at. She could confess her lie to Paul, but what would be the point? He doesn't need her confession. She imagines that long-ago dinner when their grandma told him to stop jamming his face with food, and how as everyone yelled around him he hummed quietly to himself as he finished his spaghetti. She knows if she confesses now that he will say, "That's OK," and then ask her if she's going to eat her crust.

Instead she says, "Would you like to come live with me and Hal?"

Paul shrugs. "I guess so. If you want."

It's settled between them as quickly as that. In the parking lot, Paul goes over to a streetlight, crouches down, and puts his hand on the pavement.

"Something happened here," he says. He does this a lot, a sort of mystic ESP thing, as though he sees a movie of the past playing in front of him.

"What happened?" she says.

"It was a war," he says. But that's all he will say.

At home, she lies in bed next to Hal and looks at him. She has not told him about her invitation to Paul, and for all he knows about her, he doesn't know the secrets of her face tonight: Paul, Werewolf, her darkness. Her thoughts from earlier about the werewolf feel distant and crazy, hard to parse if she were to try to repeat them now in bed, like a difficult math equation she cannot solve twice. What remains is the vague sense that what drives her to goodness is not purity, but rather some dark place that needs to mask itself, again and again.

"Hey," Hal says, and reaches out to the necklace he gave her on their last anniversary, an inlaid emerald. "Your hair is all wound up in the chain."

So it is—a dark snarl of hair knotted at the clasp—and though she picks and picks at it, the hair is wound too tightly to untangle tonight.

She turns on her side and Hal puts his arm around her. He is a good man, and he loves her, so that must be proof of something. She knows Hal will come to accept Paul's move into their home, though maybe not immediately. But Paul is hers, and Hal is hers, and so in time it will work out. And between her mantra, she thinks about the healthy meals she'll cook Paul once he moves in, and the room she's always thought of as the nursery that could be his room instead, and what color she will paint it.

This Is Who
She Was

There isn't any good place to start.

I have a picture. In the picture two women share a kitchen. Checkered floor. Wire basket of lemons.

One of the women is Ruth. I am the other. The men, hers and mine, are not in the picture. Ruth squeezes lemon juice into a blue bowl. I remember her hands were covered with paper cuts. How could a person get so many paper cuts? I didn't do anything when her hands started burning but watch her rinse them with cold water.

In my mind Ruth will always be wincing in the kitchen, squeezing lemons. I will always be watching.

* * *

The picture was taken on the night before our trip to Florida. Jay, Ruth's husband, snapped it with my camera. Their son Luke was my boyfriend. We'd only been together a few months but he'd invited me to join their family vacation. The vacation was a reunion so that Ruth could see her sisters.

"Get good sleep," Jay said. Luke's childhood bed was short; our feet hung off the end. Luke made too much noise when he pushed himself inside me. The fitted sheet came loose and bunched under my back. My necklace clasp kept snagging on the pilled polyester of the mattress.

Afterward Luke fell asleep with his fingers strumming between my legs and I moved his hand away, spread the sheet over my lap and touched myself. My finger circled a flickering pleasure, but the pleasure kept coming and going.

When I opened my eyes Luke's eyes were open and on me. Play dead. My pulse kicked in my ears. The sheet was a coil of heat in my lap, and the room was laced with the smell of our dirty sleep, like strawberry yogurt, I've always thought, never sure if it was his smell or mine. He closed his eyes again, went back to snoring. Ruth was pacing in the hallway. I knew it was Ruth because of her soft footfalls.

Later when I got up to pee she was a dark shape standing by the window at the top of the staircase. I tried to turn her into something else, coats on a coat rack or a curtain, a trick of the eye, but then her weight shifted. I hurried into the bathroom.

There was a twinge when I went pee. A hook at the end. It almost felt good.

I'd been warned about this feeling before. Urinary Tract Infection. This was the latest in a long list of incidents in this place I couldn't see or tend. When I put my fingers inside I felt nothing but a little pressure, like it wasn't really me I was touching. My insides were a collection of happenings: the first, the cyst on my left ovary. I was eleven, sleeping over in a summer girl's guest bedroom. I woke up at sunrise to a mouthful of spit, and stayed awake swallowing. That morning I went with her family to the Children's Relay at the town pool. In the deep end, the lifeguard floated saltines on the surface of the water. We were meant to swim to the crackers before they dissolved, eat the pulpy mush, and race each other back to the shallows. At the finish line all cracker was to be swallowed; they would check our mouths. I threw up in the water. The gynecologist's fingers were the first I had inside me, and then her jellied speculum.

A second cyst, so rare three interns were brought in to look. Before babies are male or female they have a duct, explained the doctor. For girls it disappears but when some vestige stays it forms a pouch. I had just read a book about a tall girl with internal male sex organs, undiscovered until a tractor accident at age fourteen. The book troubled me—the incubating clutch with its invisible hunger and hormones, and the doctor reaching inside like a magician performing a hat trick. No, nothing like that, said the doctor. You're perfectly normal.

Left ovary, said the psychic. Be careful. You might get to keep it, but it's probably best if you don't.

Twins in your family? she said.

No.

All right, she said. But there will be twins.

Bacteria. Spreading from urethra to bladder, my first UTI. The feeling was unsettling, but my mind was on Ruth, waiting by the window in the shared silence of a house put to bed. I was afraid to open the bathroom door and when I did she was gone.

My two previous boyfriends' mothers were also named Ruth. Luke's Ruth stood out in the lineup; the others had gray wiry hair, thick socks over thick ankles, bucket-like wool hats that they crocheted themselves. Both walked a large number of dogs, cleaned counters with disinfectant wipes, and made large bland batches of scrambled eggs. Of course there were differences, but these were the ways in which they were the same.

Luke's Ruth was tiny, powdered pale, with dark, tailored jackets and pants hemmed to expose a whittled inch of wrist or ankle. Her hair was a silky black tussle, and often she fixed it during conversation, her lips pursing bobby pins. I never saw her mouth without red lipstick. She wore her collarbones like jewelry.

Luke showed me postcards of her paintings, black ink swiped across huge blank canvases. Their home was full of art, but none of it was hers: sailboats on the lake, pink dabs for sailors' faces; children kicking their feet at the end of a dock; a spaniel chasing down a flock of grouse.

Luke left me alone with Ruth in the hotel room while he and Jay played a game of tennis. She poured wine into two paper cups.

"I feel slightly deranged," she said, holding her hand over her smile. There was a small gap between her front teeth. "Too many miles of yellow lines." Our paper cups pressed together in a silent cheers. We sat on the bed and sipped.

I thought maybe I would tell her about my infection, but I didn't. My discomfort stayed in the background during the first leg of the car ride. What I'd expected as we pulled onto the eight-hour stretch of highway was a repeat of my mother's lore: fifteen, she had a UTI on a road trip to drop my aunt at a psychiatric hospital. My grandmother was behind the wheel. They were driving from Maine to Virginia with cold cloths tied around their foreheads, and Chinese fans in hand. My aunt was in the passenger seat, reeling from a nervous breakdown, afraid of the radio. My grandmother drove all day and night—she would not stop. My mother's urge to pee was a plague, and the idea of relief was false, just a searing trickle. She crouched in the backseat and peed into a pickle jar. "Don't come crying to me," said my grandmother. "I know you've been sleeping around."

"I think they left us here to bond," said Ruth. "Either that or they're trying to bond. One of us will. I think we have a good chance at beating them."

But we were nervous together. The wax on my cup had softened by the second use. The paper warped beneath my fingers.

"What do you see in Luke?" she asked, just as our silence was starting to feel comfortable. I was starving, the wine slippery in my stomach.

I said he was generous, or open. Or sweet.

"I don't have an answer," I said at the end of my answer. "I just love him. I don't know why."

Another cup of wine.

"That's right," she said. "He is sweet. He's young. We all love him." She drank from the bottle and handed it to me. It was nearly empty. I put my mouth over the blot from her lipstick.

"I hope you take good care of each other."

"We will," I said. "We do."

"Lovely ladies," Jay called down the hallway. Ruth and I were punching numbers at the vending machine. Ruth kept punching DD instead of D7. She kicked the machine when it didn't release her Hershey bar.

"Easy," Jay said. "My wife the sugar junkie." His smile was seamless porcelain. He scooped her up.

"I'm famished!" she yelled. She kicked at his thighs. He opened the door and threw her on the bed.

Luke was wearing a new white Sheraton Hotel visor, and so was Jay. I wanted to make a joking gesture toward the visor, and with the same look reprimand him for leaving me alone too long, but he wouldn't look back at me. He spun the racket handle inside his palm and watched Ruth.

Jay pulled her feet into his lap and rubbed them.

"Be gentle. I broke it kicking the machine." His hands cupped her foot. Between his fingers I could see her toes wiggling.

"Here, Mom," said Luke. "Consolation prize." He pulled another matching visor from a paper bag and fit it over her delicate twist of hair. Her ears stuck out, folded by the weight of the wide white brim.

"So good to me," she said. When she tried to take it off the Velcro on the band snagged her hair. Her hands struggled at the back of her head.

"Let me," Jay said, but she yanked free before he could help and tossed the visor into my lap. "We can share it."

Strands of her hair hung from the Velcro, and I covered them with my hand.

Luke was a generous man, and a sweet man, but I do not remember much. There are still frames I can explore, with their own smells and sounds, and he prowls and paces my memory like its borders cage him.

We went back to our hotel room, adjacent to Ruth and Jay's, after dinner.

Maybe this night we stood in the shower and soaped each other's backs and chests, and when I looked at him I said in my head, *here I am, here I am, here I am,* but mostly I looked at my hand as it soaped and thought about some other thing, like when would he move aside so I could have the hot water.

Or the hotel sheets were shiny and smooth, my legs feeling wonderful because I'd shaved them and the sheets were satin.

Or that was the night he went to the bathroom and drank three glasses of water in a row, his Adam's apple bobbing up and down in his throat, and said "Will you watch it around my mom?"

I said, "What do you mean?"

"Just take it easy around her."

"What, I like her."

"Like drinking. Drinking with her."

"Why'd you never mention it before? If it worries you?"

"She never drank before," he said.

Or that night was the first night on the trip I was nauseous. I ran for the bathroom in the middle of fighting. He crouched beside me while I dry heaved, brushed one strand of hair out of my face and then another, never grabbing the whole bunch.

Because I felt sick sex that night would be off the table, and maybe that's why we curled into each other, the heat of him wrapped around me itchy as wool, my eyes on the shadowy hotel wall and its green and white stripes. We held hands and he worked his nails against my palm. The feeling gave me goose bumps at first, but his nails lost track of me, got stuck in their own rhythmic rut of scratching. And then he told me that Ruth had cancer, that she needed a hysterectomy. It did not look good, but she had time. Enough time to drink and paint all day, and to see her sisters.

Ruth didn't talk during the drive the next day. I wiped the thread of drool that hung from Luke's mouth. I listened to the brassy tap of Jay's class ring on the wheel. In Georgia, we pulled toward a sign with a painted peach. I pretended to be asleep as Jay paid for a bushel. Ruth had her head tipped to the side as though she were also asleep, but when I glanced over I could see the whites of her eyes through her dark glasses.

"For you, my Georgia peach," Jay said to her, passing the hard peaches around. Jay and I gnawed their woody white flesh, working them down to their pits. We threw the stones out the windows. Ruth nibbled hers, then peeled at its skin. Luke put his peach between us and it rolled onto the floor, where it would pinball around for days before lodging under the seat to fill the car with sweet ripening, then rotting.

* * *

The thruway to the beach house had ocean on either side. Luke woke and begged Jay to pull over. The sedan jittered onto the rumble strip. Luke pulled me out to the breezy breakdown lane.

He dashed across the street and his head dipped out of view below a mound of blown sand. I slid sideways down the plunging dune, but he was already yards ahead, tacking toward the water, so I stopped chasing and gathered his trail of stripped clothes. There were crabs everywhere, skittering in my peripheral vision, tiny curls of quicksand where they burrowed. He ran into the water and swells washed over him.

"Get in here!" he cried. My pain had returned and morphed into a diffuse throb in my pelvis, stretching awake now that we were out of the car.

I was in up to my ankles when Ruth came running from behind me, and teetered into the surf with a wild crashing and laughter, too recklessly, I worried, and she was too small, the white froth at her knees.

"Watch it, Mom!" Luke yelled. He was way out in the water, bobbing like a blond buoy. A wave was coming for her.

She was in up to her chest. It took me so long to run for her, through the water. I wrapped my arms around her waist and held tight. Her hands went up against the wall of the wave before it slammed down, pitching us apart. When I surfaced she was back in the shallows, still lipsticked, smiling loose and wide.

The beach house was crowded with aunts. They came at me with flabby arms to fold me into hugs. They had the pillowy busts of nurses. With her clothes slicked to her skin, Ruth looked like a little boy beside them, all ribs and hip bones and her tiny breasts. She flapped her collar, trying to hide the sheerness of her wet blouse. Jay squeezed her neck as though he were scruffing a kitten. My little mermaid, he called her. The aunts brought her a satin robe and she sat draped on the arm of the couch, her glass fogged by chilled white wine.

Ruth's sisters arranged that Luke and I sleep in separate beds. I stayed on the first floor, on a pullout couch in front of a television and video console. On the days it rained Luke's little cousins lay on my bed all afternoon. They left behind a dusting of sand, peeled sunburn, and chips that I'd shake from my sheet before sleeping.

Luke's bedroom was on the fourth floor. He swam in the ocean, or he tossed a Frisbee, dashing back and forth on the hot sand. He was a fast runner, and he tanned, and grew a patchy beard while I watched from the shore, achy and overwarm, my body shaded by an umbrella and wrapped in a towel. Ruth sat with me and watched the swimmers and the water.

Luke and I had sex once, in the outdoor shower while the aunts and cousins beat each other with bright foam noodles in the pool. The shower stall walls were made out of splintery compressed woodchips. It smelled the way my gerbil's cage used to smell. The water, from inside the sunning garden hose, was only warm for the first few moments. When I made a noise he put his hand over my mouth. Someone had left a hot water bottle full of sweet tea to brew on the edge of the bench inside the shower, and when I knocked the bench it flopped to the ground and wiggled there.

Lying on the couch reading with him end to end, I reached out and found his earlobe with my toes and held it. When I was little I used to thread my blanket between my toes so I could fall asleep.

We ate Cajun shrimps. Ruth sat across from me at the dinner table, picking apart her shrimp carefully while the rest of them got sauce all over their bibs.

The aunts cackled around us, stirring up bowls of different sour cream–based dips. A projector whirred overhead. Luke held me between his legs, and Jay took a picture. I still have that picture, his sunburned face next to my pallid face. Someone switched the lights off and a hazy old film began to play on the wall. The film was sped up, and the family was rushing around the campfire, storming into the lake, the teeter totter moving frantically up and down, and everywhere the aunts, as girls, in stripes and bobs, flashing smiles.

The movie was silent, but a chorus rose in the room each time a new girl stepped into the frame.

"That's me!" one aunt shrieked, and another said, "No, that's cousin Wanda, what an awful haircut. She was with us that summer. That's that yellow bathing suit, remember?" Wanda, her face a blur, dashed from the camera into the lake and dove under, but before she could surface the camera swung away. The older girls scattered and the little girls hammed into the lens, and in the distance was dark-haired, smudge-eyed Ruth in a pastel-green shirt worn as a dress. First she was leaning against the trunk of a tree with big leaves and later I caught her behind the crowded campfire, dipping plates from a white stack into a basin of water.

"Where's Ruth?" yelled the aunt who had mistaken herself for Wanda. "Ruth, do you see yourself?" But Ruth wasn't sitting on the couch where she had been. I didn't know where she had gone, and I didn't say anything about recognizing her because maybe it wasn't her after all, though I knew how she leaned into her hips and how her hair must have fallen then, limp and wavy, over one shoulder.

The film stuttered and the yellow tinge and quiet of the sixties clicked to a different reel with a downpour that sounded like a swarm of wasps. A man with a big red beard walked on-screen carrying a blond baby in a slicker, and the man was Jay, though his face was fatter, and the baby was Luke, probably two years old. Jay sat Luke on an inflatable raft inside a thin, swift stream of rainwater that ran through a flooded lawn. The baby laughed as the raft bounced on the water, away from the camera, and Ruth's voice off-screen said, "Please, don't hurt my baby, don't hurt my baby." Whoever was behind the camera had a low laugh that shook everything.

And then the scenes kept changing. In one there was cake, and dated poufs of hair in scrunchies, a woman with acid-washed jeans scooping ice cream. I realized I was going to be sick.

The upstairs hallway was carpeted and dark, and, away from the shrieking family, I could hear the waves coming in. Outside it was raining, harder and harder against the window. I put my hand to my mouth and bolted for the bathroom and there was Ruth, sloshing to cover herself in the tub.

"Oh my dear," she said as I retched. "Oh my dear heart."

The shrimp, I tried to say, but I couldn't. I breathed and breathed the green smell of her bath's steam. Ruth climbed from the tub to hold back my hair, her nails circling my shoulder blade. When I stood the knees of my jeans were wet.

"Take my bathwater," she said, toweling. "While it's still hot."

The pain nested inside my pelvis, an unrelenting ache, throbbing and tunneling. When I got into the warm water it felt better.

"You going to make it?" Her cheeks were swollen and stippled red. She was an ugly crier, like me.

"Yeah."

"Splash your face," she said. Her eyes were bright with mothering.

"I don't know why I didn't tell you before," I said between splashes. "I knew I had a UTI. But then it went away."

"Is there pain now?"

I nodded.

She sat on the edge of the tub, brushing off the sole of one foot and then the other before putting them in the water

174

beside my legs. Scars webbed her knees and she caught me looking.

"When you're pregnant, your center of gravity keeps changing. I didn't know that, they don't tell you that, unless you're an athlete or something. I was working in the city, and the sidewalk between our apartment and my studio was uneven, and I tripped almost every day. All my tights had holes at the knees and Jay would dress my knees with Band-Aids. I was like an eight-year-old boy."

I pictured Ruth at my age, hurrying in a trench coat and French twist, scabs under her tights, the sidewalk invisible beneath the dome of her belly. It was a comfort to picture her.

I found Luke under the blankets on my pullout bed, and climbed in with him to tell him about the UTI. I could feel that he hadn't wiped the sand and crumbs from the sheet before getting under. He was sad, and he didn't know why.

"I'm sorry you're sick." He put his head on my stomach.

"You stay," Ruth said to Luke, as she bundled me in her scarf before we left for the hospital. It was ninety degrees out but my teeth chattered. "No offense, sweetie, but you'll get in the way." She kissed the top of his head.

Nothing went like it was supposed to. I was trying to be in love with Luke, but we were stranger and stranger, like the smoothly twirling top that begins to lurch and wobble in loose circles.

* * *

When the doctor saw me he said, "Are you sexually active?"

"Yes," I said.

"Within the past week?"

"Yes."

"With the same partner?"

"Well, there was that one wild night," I said, and listened to my laugh trail off. "No, no, just the one partner." Maybe it was the fever that made me joke. The only other man on the vacation was Jay. Ruth's hands folded one way and then another, an arrangement in her lap. She had followed me from the waiting room without asking, and stayed quiet and small in the corner. I had thought maybe she would hold my hand.

The hospital rooms were overflowing, so after the doctor saw me they wheeled my gurney into the hall and Ruth trailed alongside, her arm linking my IV stand. My teeth were still chattering, and my whole body ached. They gave me anti-nausea medication and an IV of saline, which was cold as it flowed into my arm.

Somehow between the fever peaking, the doctor, and the gurney, I think, I'm not certain, that Ruth got drunk and sad. My hospital gown was open at the back. When I fell asleep, I turned onto my side, and woke in fear of the hallway's drifters spying my underpants with no Ruth to guard me. I didn't know where she'd gone. An old man with deflated nakedness under his gown shuffled past wailing, "Martha!" The IV leashing him tugged from his arm and he weaved untethered, trailing neat drops of blood into the hallway's crowd.

Far away down the hall was Ruth, tiny inside her tailored clothes, their crisp lines wilting in the heat, purse strap slipping from her shoulder, her hair wispy and undone. Compared to her I felt moonfaced, wide-palmed, a sturdy girl, and a plain one with plain sadness. The doctor was walking toward me, and he reached me before Ruth did. His drawl made him sound amused. His big, soft hand patted mine. He drawled slow, but Ruth moved slow, and he fit it all in before she could reach me. Click, a key turned inside me as he mouthed about the baby, dumbly obvious as he spoke it aloud, growing inside me. The kidney infection and the baby, and the one could hurt the other, but we caught it in time, he said, and it was so early in my pregnancy that the risk was very low with a course of antibiotics.

"Don't you worry. Your baby'll be just fine," he said, rushing elsewhere.

Ruth was so small in the breeze of her drunkenness. It swayed her.

"Can't keep secrets in this place," she said. Each syllable dragged. "I see big news all over your face. Let me up."

She climbed onto my gurney. I tried to rearrange my expression but it was no use, I felt it telling things to Ruth. In hindsight I was feverish, but I knew then that she was like a psychic, seeing it all, my bumps and hollows and innards and growths. I told her I was pregnant.

She curled against me. Her sigh was warm and wet, sharp-smelling. Her head was a nice weight on my shoulder.

"Luke had a twin who died," she said. "In utero. I was still pregnant with him for three more weeks, waiting for Luke to be born."

I smoothed her hair, trailing my IV cord.

"I spoke to my belly like that baby was still alive. I couldn't picture him gone inside me. I thought the sadness would kill me." Everyone was fast, wheeling around us. No time to stare, they had spills to mop. "But then my beautiful Luke was born."

A long time later she said, "Luke's a wonderful boy, but he's a baby. He's not at all ready to be a dad." It was advice, and I needed a woman's advice. She put her hand into her purse and worked it around in there for a minute, two minutes, fishing for lipstick. She drew the red bow of her mouth perfectly, but capped the lipstick without screwing it back down.

"Fuck," she said. Our bodies made little noises on the sheath of tissue paper that lined the gurney.

I was supposed to crave pickles, and sauerkraut, and have the kind of husband who would pick up jars of these things at the corner store in the middle of the night, and stay up with me while I ate, rubbing my stomach with cool lotion. I was supposed to have long hair, and a wide, wise mouth, and to have read many more books, traveled, married with a flower garland and a backless silk dress, taught in tweed coats with elbow patches, spooned my husband and taken long baths with him, and I was supposed to have seen my own mother, frail and stooped, through many years of sickness with grace and patience, and be cauterized by the pain of losing her, and turned bright and still and steady inside, like a mother should be, and then I'd be a mother.

I've imagined Ruth and me together, in Maine, in a cabin by the bay. Ruth, pacing the floor in a painter's shirt, like the one I took from my grandmother's bureau after she died, long and pilled, stiff where the paint streaked. Ruth's smile, too wide, a baby bouncing on her shoulder. Her clear steady voice rings through my vision, guides the baby into sleep.

I left Florida the next day. I told Luke I was too sick to stay, and this was true. They had me on all kinds of antibiotics. Ruth hugged me at the airport and she didn't say anything, or look at me in any special kind of way, which made me wonder if it was possible she was so out of it at the hospital that she'd forgotten I was pregnant. Luke and I didn't make the effort to see each other again that summer. Whatever we had slipped away easily, just a summer fling. Luke phoned a couple times but I didn't return his calls, and I didn't go back to school in the fall. Rumor never got around to Luke as it might have if I lived in a town that was closer to our college, but I don't, and it didn't.

The three women I knew who killed themselves were all grandmothers.

The first, a ketchup heiress who lived in a yellow mansion with a wraparound porch. On warm nights her grandchildren slept outside in hammocks.

The second, a middle school Spanish teacher. She ate homemade granola for breakfast, coiled a braid around her head, fell in love late in life, and married in the entryway of her barn. She was bustling and red cheeked, always dancing.

And Ruth, with her lipstick and elegant tapered fingers and the scars on her knees, who walked into the water.

I stayed at home and lay in bed in the room above my parents' garage, waiting for my stomach to grow. It didn't for the longest time, and then it was enormous.

My center of gravity changed every day, and I fell on the way to the post office. My mom dressed my bloody knee.

All winter I lay on my back and watched the dead spider with her egg sack and her scrap of web blowing between the panes in the storm window, and in the spring her front legs began to squirm and my two gentle girls were born.

Changeling

I rode the bus away from Gray. He thought I was going on a trip, but I knew I was beginning the long-drawn-out sorrow of leaving him, even though I'd send postcards from Boston and return to him in a week, slipping my hand into his jeans pocket on the ride home from the bus stop, his face so startlingly sweet and shaved for my return, the familiar smell of his neck lulling me into the first sleep I'd had in days.

There was a woman on the bus with my mother's face, humping an oversized backpack up the aisle in Augusta. I hadn't seen my mother in nineteen years. She left us when I was four, met a new man, joined the military. I pretended not to recognize her, and she pretended not to know me, and got a seat in the back of the bus.

At the Portland bus stop the bus driver lumbered up the aisle, counting passengers for reboarding to ensure no one snuck on unticketed. The numbers were off. I handed over my receipt from my coat pocket, where I'd fingered its edges until they were soft and blue tinged with smudged ink.

The problem passenger, of course, was the woman who might be my mother. Her voice was deep and gravelly as the bus driver questioned her, her mumbled answers lost in the commotion of the bus. She didn't have my mom's voice, as I remembered it. Mom's bright singing had won her blue-colored shots at karaoke. Like Tammy Wynette.

I watched the woman with my mother's face and watched everyone else watching her. She wore an orange hunting cap. Her hair was blonde and thin. She had the haircut of a teenage boy who insists on keeping his hair long and trimming it himself, limp curls cropped unevenly above her shoulders. She wore an army jacket. It was not the handsome, brass-buttoned suit in the portrait she'd sent me from her military days. She wore army pants too, green, wool maybe, that hung low on her hips, which were as narrow as a boy's. She had the same ruddy, unwrinkled skin as my mother, though she was a good twenty pounds lighter, her hair a few shades darker. They shared a bone structure—pointed chin, prominent cheekbones. She covered her teeth when she smiled sorrowfully at the bus driver, just like my mother had done. Mom's teeth came in crooked and stained, and my teeth grew the same. I was raised in the time of fluoride and orthodontics, but I had her bad genes, drank well water, couldn't afford braces. All my friends had straight white smiles. It's unsettling—a beautiful young woman with a smile like a witch.

I was convinced the mother-stranger riffling through her pockets for her ticket was once beautiful. Why else be ashamed of that smile? It suited the rest of her now, but she hid it from habit. Mom once had the trappings of beauty in a replicable way—fake nails, bleach blonde hair, thick makeup. Fresh from the shower she looked frightened and alien, her face like an underdeveloped Polaroid.

She moved on to tearing apart her backpack, an enormous, camo-patterned thing with a frame, and still she couldn't come up with the receipt, so she began unpacking carefully folded undershirts, underpants, and balls of yellow socks, stacking them in the center isle. It was winter, and the aisle was gritty, and wet with slush. Two plastic bags, one full of sandwiches, one full of orange peels. A handful of tissues. One of the sock balls rolled away from her, disappearing under the seats.

"That's it," she said, raising her voice, "that and feminine stuff, which stays in the bag. I bought a ticket, in Bangor, like I told you. You don't remember me? Not one of you remembers?" And then she was talking at all of us, and we stopped watching her and pretended to be occupied with our magazines or the view of the parking lot. "You, sir," she said, pointing. "I sat right there in front of you. Tell the driver." But the man said nothing.

I raised my hand. "I saw her," I said.

"Well, why the heck didn't you say so earlier?" she asked. "But thank you. Thank you, sweetheart."

Now that she was one of us again, a lady leaned over in her seat to help her collect her clothes from the aisle.

"I need some air, sir," the woman said.

"Ma'am, we're behind schedule as is," said the bus driver, wheezing his way back to his seat, cheeks pinked.

"Listen now, everyone else on this bus got to get off and breathe a sec while I was fussing with you. I need to stretch my legs." So the doors thwacked open, and the cold air came pouring in, and he left the doors open like he was proving something while she paced the parking lot, throwing punches, stretching like a boxer. When she lifted her arms over her head I glimpsed her stomach, bisected by a scar.

"I'm sitting with the nice one," she said when she reboarded. I moved my purse from the seat beside me. I couldn't possibly look at her face this close up. She smelled both animal and floral.

"Here," she said. "Have some nice potpourri, homemade by my ma." What I thought were orange peels were orange rose petals, stuffed in a sandwich bag. She crushed the bag against my chest and I thanked her, dreading the thought of her smell leaching into my things.

It was three o'clock, but nearly dark outside, and the bus headlights sparkled against the ice-encased birches. Whole swaths of trees were bowed down with the weight of the ice, like a forest in the wake of a nuclear blast.

"Little of this too?" she said, reaching into her long, deep pocket, pulling out a fifth of Coffee Brandy. I was already tipsy. Gray took me to Ruby Tuesday's before the bus stop. He bought me two coral-colored drinks to celebrate my trip, peach schnapps something with fruit bits floating in it. I was afraid the bus driver would catch us and kick us both off the bus, but I was even more afraid of her. I took the bottle in the darkness, toasted to my mother, and drank.

Mom used to park the car in the driveway and drink. Watching the house, watching me jump on the trampoline. When she drove away and didn't come back Dad ripped off all his clothes and went running naked through the woods, branches cutting him up. After that he joined a Christian cult where the men wore bowler hats and the women wore dresses made from curtains and listening to the radio was forbidden. He told me I was a sinner, and I moved in with my grandfather. I played the radio all night under my covers.

I used to see Mom everywhere, blonde hair swishing through crowds away from me. She sent me postcards from Tallahassee and Honolulu, from Eau Claire, Wisconsin. All they said was "I love you." One day the postcards stopped. The military had discharged her for bad conduct. She just disappeared. At the playground behind my house I crawled into strange women's laps, snuck into their brood of children, slipped my hand, unnoticed, into theirs. I can remember how the startled mothers' expressions rearranged when they discovered it was my hand they held—a look of pity mixed, consistently, with repulsion. No one wants a changeling.

Buses got me thinking. I closed my eyes and pictured Gray and me in a bath together, lit candles and peace of mind. I'd grown up to be a real woman. And then I pictured my secret self, a self that diminished and diminished until I didn't exist at all, and I had no one to love. My face turned gaunt and sallow. I stopped looking in mirrors.

"All these fancy folks," she said, "and nobody notices me. Isn't that the way. Well, you must be a good looker." She leaned in close, and I looked at her through the darkness, headlights sweeping her face.

"I mean, what do these people know? I've got a sick ma, I spend all Christmas trying to get her out of that darned trailer, come up to Boston with me. I'm just trying to get me some sleep on this bus, and this world's just got to stick its finger in it. You know what I mean."

I wanted to tell her she was loud, that people were looking, that we might get caught, but I was too nervous around her to think. I swallowed more brandy. My mouth was dry.

"Your mom's sick?" I said.

"Sick as they come."

We passed the brandy back and forth, sweet as syrup, and I drank each time she passed it to me against my better judgment, even though better judgment reigned in my life at that time, an organizing principle that seemed to make my decisions for me. After the first couple swallows the brandy no longer made me gag, and *this is it*, I thought, the moment when I cross to the other side of the mirror, to a path where leaving Gray was inevitable and I could get trashed on a bus with this mother, who drained the bottle and slipped her hand into mine.

"Where you wanna sleep?" she slurred when the bus pulled into South Station. They were unloading suitcases, and I spotted mine, blue with a bright-pink luggage tag, pulled to the curb. It was strange to see my pink tag, bought special for this trip, and it reminded me of so much that already seemed far behind me: Gray, the nursing conference, my booked hotel room, my home. I tripped down the aisle. I could barely move my legs. In those days I was one of those drinkers who could usually conceal their drunkenness. I was going to say drunks, but I'm not.

"I'm no dyke or anything," she said, jamming her hands into her back pockets, rocking on her heels. "But if you need a place to land, you're welcome."

"I shouldn't," I said.

"Who's judging?"

"You got a nice place?" She grabbed my bag from me and wheeled it through the station. I wondered who was watching us, but no one was. Most city people are hardly ever watching. I took out my cell phone and fumbled with it, thinking I should do something about Gray, but she was charging ahead of me. I didn't want to lose sight of her hunting hat in the crowd, and anyway my eyes couldn't focus on the text message from Gray that was up on the screen. I closed one eye, trying to read. Gray would call me seven times that night, wanting to know I made it in safe. He'd call the hotel, growing frantic when they said I never checked in. The next morning I'd try to soothe with half-truths: how I ran into an old friend, went out drinking, slept over. It all sounded blatantly like an affair.

We waited together on the subway platform, beside a movie poster where someone had blacked out all the actors' eyes with marker. The cool, acrid breeze of the approaching train blew our hair.

She hung from the train's handrail like it was a monkey bar. Her shirt rode up, and again I tried not to look at her stomach, at that long, pink scar.

"I love to stretch, you know? Keep fit. You don't keep fit, you die." Other people glanced at her as she swung. "That's my ma's problem. Sitting in that chair all day, falling asleep with her cigarette burning. She's asking for it. Cigarette falls and she burns herself. She's got scars all over her chest." She laughed. Every time she laughed she coughed, phlegmy and raw. I could see myself reflected in the dark train window across the aisle. For a moment I pretended that she wasn't with me, and that I was in league with every other polite commuter—work-weary women, tight lipped, in their black or gray coats, with their hands on the mouths of their purses.

"So what's your problem?" she said.

When I didn't acknowledge her she just asked me louder, swinging into the seat beside me.

"I don't have a problem," I said. When I'm drunk I have a hard time meeting people's eyes, so I studied her stained white high tops. The shoes must have been one size too small, her big toes straining the fabric. I looked at her mouth. My mom's front teeth had these tiny chips at the bottom, because when she was little she'd chew on bottle caps. This woman's teeth didn't have any chips.

I knew if I were a stranger on the train watching the two of us, I would think she was a homeless woman bothering a nice young girl. *Maybe that's true,* I thought. *Maybe there's no home waiting on the other end of the train.* I tried to conjure fear, her eerie, familiar face looming close, but fear had drained from me. I lifted my arm and let it flop heavily back into my lap. This was a test of drunkenness I'd always enjoyed, since I was fifteen and stole two swallows of lemon vodka from my grandpa's cabinet. I lay in bed afterward, lifting my hand and letting it fall, my heavy head lolling on the pillow.

"She's gone quiet on me, folks," she said, but this time her voice was low, just for us. She had a spitty way of enunciating her words that drinkers I've known share.

"So you've got a nice place?" I said.

"Well, it's a work in progress. But I'd stay there all day if I could. I'm worse than Ma about my house. My house is the only thing in my life that hasn't betrayed me."

"I'm sorry to be rude," I said, "but I forgot your name."

"Here we're having a sleepover and you don't even know my name. It's Cheryl. Try and remember this time. Like cherry."

"Like cherries," I repeated. I couldn't recall her telling me her name. My mother's name was Flora, is Flora, if she's still alive. People called her Flor. She hated the nickname. "I mop floors," she said. "My name is flowers." I imagined Mom would like to be renamed Cherry. I thought how I would like a name like that, if only for one night. My name is plain Dora. Door. I imagined knotting a cherry stem with my tongue.

The train lurched back and forth, yanking our bodies. It seemed to be going faster than it should, stations whipping past in seconds, faces blurred. I wondered if the train operator ever went rogue, skipping stops in the dark, dead-end tunnel.

Cheryl had a real house. It was brick and squat, half-covered in dead climbing vine. The lawn was gravel but there was a garden plot, and inside the garden plastic plant containers, the plant's yellowed leaves spilling out over the snow. There was a swan planter in the garden, its long neck ringed with rust. Bars on the windows, and behind them shadows and flickering light. A face appeared in the window and then disappeared again behind the orange curtain.

Her home was not what I'd expected. I expected a sort of homelessness within a home, yanked-up carpet and leaky ceilings, boxes of delusional junk—plastic horses, clown ashtrays, thirty packs of mop heads—stacked to the ceilings. In reality her home was cold and spotless, lit by scented candles. There was a plastic cover over the couch, and I could see evidence of recent vacuuming in the weft of the carpet. She kept lovebirds, but their cage was clean. One of them made a soft cooing noise in its sleep.

"Make yourself comfortable," she said, handing me a glass of scotch that burned my eyes when I drew it near my face. The plastic couch covering crinkled beneath us. From the living room doorway, a teenage boy tipped his baseball cap.

"Good you're back," he said. "Dalia was getting weird without you." He picked at chipped paint on the doorframe, peeling off a single, long strip.

"Good to be back," she said. "Quit that. Come meet my friend."

"Nah, happy to meet you but excuse me. I've got some stuff going," and he bowed away, his stomps on the stairs creaking the roofline.

"That's your son?" I said.

She snorted, then was seized by the same gravelly laughter, slapping my thigh, wiping her eyes. "It's OK. The first time I seen Tony, I thought he was a little boy, too."

Tony came back downstairs. His pants were halfway down his hips and he wore a peach windbreaker that swished when he walked. His hair was shiny with gel, glistening in the candlelight. He was maybe four feet tall if he was lucky, but I noticed that his chest and neck were thick with muscle. He had four travel bottles of Listerine in his hand, one between each finger, that he cracked open and poured over ice.

"Go on, Tony. Tell her how old you are."

"Sweet sixteen," he said.

"Yeah, keep telling yourself that." She leaned into me, and said against my ear, "Don't you worry about the mouthwash. Tony's out of his mind, but his mind wasn't so good to begin with. He's set on drinking that swill. I just wish he'd buy the big bottles then, they're cheaper. But it's travel bottles. I don't think he's going nowhere." He swished the drink around his mouth, ignoring her. She raised her voice. "I said, I don't think you're going nowhere, baby."

"I have ears, Cher," Tony said. "Cheers, ladies." He drained his glass, and I thought of tiny Toulouse-Lautrec, his absinthe, his women. "Keeps me fresh," he said. "And sane. Sure beats lighter fluid."

"There's booze here, Tony, as always," said Cheryl. "For adults. That rot gut's killing you."

"Not fast enough." He closed his eyes and rocked his Barcalounger back, pulling an afghan up over his head.

At this point I wasn't doing so well. It hit me quick. I kept taking little nips of the scotch. I thought about the hotel I never checked into, a bed all my own and white noise, and talking sweet to Gray before sleep. How I could have woken up in the morning, put on a hotel robe and made myself tea, turned the blinds so the light poured in. At this point it felt like I'd never slip into a nicely made bed again, never cup my hands around a hot tea. Like Gray wouldn't ever love me again.

Gray's the nicest man. He found a baby mouse under the seat of his truck, and made a whole thing for her, tunnels and tufts of sawdust. He called her Miss Mouse, and petted her with his pinky finger, this big, biker-type guy. He bought me my pink luggage tags. It was easy to think I loved him. I poured myself more drink.

Leaving Gray was the worst thing I could think of, and I was leaning into that darkness. It's like what I wanted in sex. I got turned on imagining terrible things, the opposite of what I wanted in real life. I would fantasize Gray addicted to heroine. I would fantasize Gray was my grandfather. These images started a tiny, lustful engine chugging away inside me.

"Don't mind Tony," whispered Cheryl. "He's a son of a bitch, but he had to get that way. Kids picked him apart at school. Even now, a grown man, and people still start stuff with him all the time. You see this," she said, lifting her shirt, pointing at the long, pink scar. "I took a knife for Tony. Some-one's trying to kill Tony, they're going to have to kill me." There were little snores coming from beneath the blanket.

"How do you know him?"

She raised her eyebrows. "Up, down, and sideways. Tony's my man. I've known that sucker every way there is." I pictured her, stalking the streets behind Tony like a bodyguard. I pictured her kneeling down to kiss him. From a distance, they would look like two men kissing, like a man kissing a boy.

"But how'd you meet him?"

"Oh, a lot of strays come through here. I got a house, right? Kids that can't take care of themselves. I had this kid here last month, real faggoty type— excuse me, I'm not preju-dice, but this kid had tits. Real nice kid though, really sad. He wouldn't even sleep on a bed, he just wrapped himself up in blankets on the floor. Kicked them all out though, to make way for my ma."

"Am I one of your strays?" I said.

"I don't know, are you?"

I could feel my eyes drifting all around. She wasn't so much like my mom.

"You wanna put on some music?" I said.

"Not now, sweetie. With Tony sleeping."

"I can take care of myself. Are you calling me sweetie because you think you have to take care of me?"

"Sure I do. But I called you sweetie because you're sweet, that's all."

"Yeah," I said, the room spinning. I got up and opened doors, trying to find the bathroom but I kept finding broom closets instead, and bedrooms that smelled of strange bodies, all the kids she'd kept and let loose. When I found the bathroom, I flipped at the switch but no light came on. I lay down on the cool tile, no lunch and no dinner, my stomach clenched and hot with scotch. Some time later she flicked on the light and sat beside me, pressing her warm palm to my forehead. I couldn't move my legs to stand, or open my eyes. The room spun.

"You're OK, little girl," she said. "What did I do to you? Baby in the big city, and I get her wrecked." She slung my arm over her shoulder. "Up we go, that's it."

I caught sight of my reflection, my face streaked with mascara. Every day I had nice, quiet thoughts. Kept my shadow self at bay. She was there, in the mirror. Frenzied and dangerous, her body a cloud of buzzing beetles.

"Let's get you in bed, now," she said, leading me by my shoulders through the house, which felt overly big, like a house in a dream, full of long, dark, cold hallways that went on and on. "Let's give you Ma's room. There we are," she said. I lay back on the quilted bed, my throat and chest and stomach raw.

"You look like my mom," I said. "I thought you were her."

"Me?" She propped me up, made me take a sip of water. "That's a kicker. How old do you think I am?"

"Mom's age," I said.

"How old are you, kiddo?"

"Twenty-three," I said.

"Well I'm thirty-three. May not look it, but the city will do that. So if I'm your mom we're in worse shape than I thought. Take another swallow."

I was crying. "I wish it was you," I said.

"It is me," she said. "Cool it now, you're OK." But something was unlocking inside me. I'm a crying kind of drunk, fine one minute, undone the next by sadness that I can't name, fierce and fast rising like floodwaters.

"Shut up." She lay down next to me. "I'm right here. I'm her." She put her hand on my waist. "I'm her. I'm right here."

Sometime in the night I remember reaching for her. I was dreaming about her. In the dream Miss Mouse was tiny again, and Cheryl cupped her in her hands.

"Quit that out," she said, turning away from me in her sleep, but she stayed, her warm back pressed against mine until morning.

I didn't want to leave the bed. I wanted to live in Cheryl's ma's room forever. Cheryl was gone and it was bright out. The street below was alive with traffic sounds, but inside the bedroom was cool and quiet. There was a crucifix above the headboard, and lacquered paintings of Jesus and the Virgin Mary over the dresser. The dresser was covered in dolls and doilies. The bedroom was different from the rest of the house, and I wondered if it was done up to make Cheryl's ma feel at home. I felt like my hangover was terminal, and I would never feel like myself again.

I found Tony in the kitchen, eating a plate of sausages with a knife. His hair was slicked back neatly, but his face looked warmed over, gray circles and bags under his eyes, deep wrinkles, and I realized he was older than I'd thought, forty maybe, fifty even.

"You look like hell," he said.

"You, too," I said.

"Well I've been there. What's your excuse?" He speared a sausage. "Cheryl's at work. Left you a twenty in case, and some lemon bars in that Ziploc. Or you can stay, she said. Woman's a saint." I made myself some tea, and held its warmth in my hands, watching the steam. "A saint," he said again. "I swear I'd be lost if she hadn't picked me," he said. "I'd be a goner."

A little girl padded into the kitchen. She had on one enormous bunny slipper, and she skidded across the linoleum to the fridge, pushing off with her bare foot, using her single slipper like an ice skate. She took out orange juice, drank from the mouth of the carton.

"Dalia, this is a nice lady. Nice lady, this is Dalia."

"She's your daughter?" I said.

"Last I checked. Cheryl's and mine."

She skated over to Tony and buried her face in the front of his shirt. "Come here, booger," he said, squeezing her. She had a mess of dark hair. I reached out and put my hand on the back of her head. There were snarls nested under her curls.

"Cheryl's at work?" I said.

"Yep. Lobster pound, twelve hours a day. She's the one who sticks those little bands on 'em. Those suckers cut her up good." For all I'd inspected her, I'd never noticed her hands.

It wasn't until I'd paid the taxi driver at the hotel that I realized I didn't know where Cheryl's house was, couldn't even remember which station she was close to. Her train was on the way to Braintree, I know, because I had pictured a brain, its folds like a winding maze, gently afloat in clear, pink water.

I never found Cheryl again, but I looked for her—broad shoulders like my mom, my mom's anxious laugh, her army green—and sometimes, many times, I thought for a second I spotted her. I searched the faces of the women in the motel parking lot by my apartment, the hookers and drug addicts. They stared right back like they knew me, all thinking I wanted something from them, all of them familiar.

Homecoming

I moved back to my hometown with my husband, which was my first mistake. Actually at that point he wasn't my husband, though we're married now. I wanted to be claimed as a wife for the sake of my own tenuous survival. In those early days in Maine, I often envisioned walking into the bay, but that sounds more poetic and energetic than what I really felt. Mostly I wanted to slip down the shower drain or hibernate for the next five years until I was prepared to be a wife and mother, and was used to the fact that all my friends lived elsewhere and it was just me and Bruce making meal after meal and eating them on the couch for the rest of our lives.

Right after the move I started to wash my face with oil, thinking that since I was back in rural Maine I should milk goats and throw away my harsh facial soap. The oil cleansing covered my face with tiny bumps that I spent hours researching online. My research suggested that the phase I was in was generally considered a purging phase so I kept washing with the oil through fall, until the texture of my skin was completely altered. In my phone's photo album, hundreds of pictures of my own face, taken to document the purge, replaced pictures of friends and beaches and Bruce and me on mountain summits.

These were the pastimes of that fall—the oil, and watching a show about brides-to-be trying on wedding dresses while Bruce worked at a wine shop where they'd get him drunk sampling wines and then he'd drive the hour back to my town weaving. The couple of times I got up the courage to confront him about being drunk he hadn't actually been drinking. I wasn't any good at telling the difference between Bruce sober and not, and he'd seemed drunk to me.

For exercise and sunlight I dressed each afternoon in a pair of men's jeans that I imagined a Maine farming woman might wear, slathered my erupting skin with makeup, and braided my hair so I could walk to the end of the driveway and collect the Rite Aid flyers from our mailbox.

When I envisioned my wedding I saw my bare feet, walking up a petal-strewn path. I would carry a bouquet of blue-bells. The weekend after we arrived in Maine Bruce planned a surprise for my birthday, a surprise he told my family about and described to me as "an elephant," and I felt sure and sharp in my chest that the surprise was a proposal. We drove four hours, my mouth dry imagining how the proposal might play out, and then he untied my blindfold in the parking lot of the

University of Maine at Fort Kent, where an upright bassist was to perform all six of the Bach cello suites.

I had mentioned to Bruce that I liked the cello suites, which I did, but I'd only heard them once and basically I just liked the cello more than other instruments, like trumpets or flutes, which I didn't like at all. The second surprise was that the bassist, who was playing by memory, forgot his place and had to search his mind for the next notes in front of the few of us gathered in the tiny auditorium, which during the day was a science classroom, as evidenced by the periodic table of elements above the stage. The bassist sent the professor who introduced him running backstage while he stood clutching his bass, and once the music stand was set up and the book of sheet music propped open precariously before him he closed his eyes and resumed playing for one lovely, sonorous second before the score flipped of its own accord to the wrong page. The audience knew this had happened but the bassist did not. When he opened his eyes there was nothing for him to do but stop playing to hunt for the correct, lost page, while we sat watching. It went on like this all the way through 136 minutes of cello suites, and afterward he struggled the bass offstage. Bruce and I went out to Applebee's, where I ordered a burger even though I'd been a vegetarian for years and we talked about the lesser mistakes the bassist had made, which even I, without knowing the Bach cello suites or classical music, found obvious—whole swaths of music were missing, or improperly timed.

* * *

Back then I woke up every morning and looked out the window at the empty driveway of our subdivision and then rubbed the soles of my feet on the soft deer hide my parents had gifted us, receiving from it the kind of comfort one might get patting a dog. With each passing day I wondered when I would feel returned to myself. The days got dark earlier, and I got out of bed later, stopped eating meals when Bruce wasn't around, and often changed from my pajamas at dusk, knowing he would be back soon. Then in early October a red Jeep went cruising by. I remembered a similar red Jeep from when I was little and living across town in the big yellow house that I had started referring to as my parents' house instead of as my home, because now my home was meant to be the prefab Cape house I shared with Bruce. Whenever I called my parents' house my home Bruce corrected me.

A summer girl named Nancy had driven the red Jeep twenty years before, which caused a stir in our two-hundred-person town where nobody drove a red car with the top down, and mostly nobody was young. I remembered her as prim and polite, her hair wet from a fresh permanent that smelled like fruit and poison, helping me onto the back of a fire truck at the Fourth of July lobster bake. I was six years old. When she graduated college, her sorority picture was printed in the summer paper—she wore a black velvet cloth draped over her shoulders and white pearls. Her tiny hands were cupped beneath her chin. She looked like a president's wife.

The story of Nancy's accident made its way back to our town in small portions. She lived in New York City after college, working as a consultant and carrying a leather Coach briefcase. Her muggers hit her over the back of the head. She was found barefoot—the muggers had stolen her shoes —and unconscious, and stayed in a coma for six days. When she woke up she was different. She spat the hospital Jell-O across the room. She sat for hours on the roof of her building smoking. Work was impossible—she often trailed off midsentence, her ears rang incessantly. She developed vertigo and during these spells would sit in the middle of the sidewalk, or on the shoulder of the street. Twice the police picked her up for public intoxication. Her friends told her she was more fun than she had been before. She slept during the day, and walked New York neighborhoods at night, wearing a man's fedora, drinking from a flask. When people trailed too close behind her, she'd yell at them, in the voice of a tiny woman who was about to transform into a hulk, "Get away," as though they were the ones that needed protection from her. She went to Coney Island and rode the log flume over and over, without her protective helmet. She came out as a lesbian, and wore a shark tooth necklace she'd bought on vacation in Costa Rica every day. Her mom stayed with her in New York for three months, setting up a prayer shrine at the kitchen table, before convincing Nancy to move back to California with her, where she spent her disability money on Ring Pops, nitrous oxide canisters, three-piece suits, and a guinea pig named Petal. Some days all she could do was lie in bed, letting the guinea pig root through her hair, trying to make a nest.

She was thirty-five. She could feed herself and dress herself and she wanted to live unsupervised and not be treated like a child. She took her guinea pig and the red Jeep—which at this point had a rusted-out undercarriage and a sunroof jammed open by one-eighth of an inch, enough to let in rain—and returned to the vacation house alone. Her parents owned a gazebo by the water with glass windows looking out in all watery directions and seagulls squawking and shitting on the roof, as they would on the roof of a lobster boat. This is where Nancy slept, on a futon on the floor, surrounded by the unearthed vestiges of her childhood—the oversized rabbit pillow with long white hair that shed all over her pajamas, the pilled Ninja Turtles comforter, the lava lamp, the porcelain kittens with blue jewels for eyes—objects she had long ago packed away into the basement for the day her children might want them.

Most of this I would learn later. On that day in October all I saw was the Jeep and the flash of her hair, which had been brown and was now bleach blonde, nearly white. I spent an hour in the bathroom with the oils and a new kind of powder makeup, applying samples, until I had tried on Beige Neutral and Sandy Fair and Sun-kissed Medium, writing notes about each on Post-its that I stuck to the bathroom mirror. Then I thought I might try to clean the toilet, but I had forgotten to buy a toilet brush. I dug through my office, which was simply a room where we hid our unpacked boxes, until I found a penny whistle that Bruce had given me as a stocking stuffer last Christmas. I wrapped the whistle in a plastic bag and used it to push a tissue around the toilet basin. As I did this I played the rehearsal track for the hundred-person choral group I had joined in an effort to make new friends. We met once a week in a church basement three towns over to sing songs in Old English that I memorized by ear. The rehearsal track was sung by the choral director, a spunky soprano with bracelets that clattered on her wrists, but she recorded the contralto part with her pitch artificially deepened and slowed. I belted out the one line I had memorized because the lyrics sounded like, "Lay out your Levi's, lustily," and pictured someone who looked good in Levi's taking them off and folding them carefully on my bed. The voice on the recording sounded like a demon being melted by sunshine.

When I finally made it to the end of my driveway I opened the mailbox and there wasn't even a flyer, just a birthday postcard from my dentist forwarded from my old address for the twenty-fifth birthday I'd celebrated two months before. I decided to keep walking along the shoulder of the road toward the harbor. When a car came by, which they did on this road at about sixty-five miles per hour, I stepped from the gravelly shoulder into the ditch and collected the garbage littered there, until the garbage was too much to hold. I was still miles away from the dock so I stacked the Burger King bags, Miller Lite cans, and Styrofoam shreds in a neat little pile and left it behind.

I had read Stephen King's memoir about life in Maine to try and feel rooted in my own life, and it comforted me to know that he too had gone for long, dangerous walks along the road's shoulder. Stephen had been hit by a van that veered into the wrong lane while the driver tried to control his Rottweiler. I imagined the same wild driver was still behind the wheel, careening down this very road with his slobbery Rottweiler as I slogged through the stream of ditch water.

I was ten minutes from my parents' house, but I didn't want them to see me. We had a deal that though we lived in the same town we would keep our lives separate unless I invited them over or they invited me over for dinner parties, which happened about twice a month, or sometimes we met in the adjacent town for a sandwich. When I met with them I wore a pair of bright, salmon-colored pants, tied my hair in a ponytail, and talked about the choir, trying to act as though everything was all right. I knew that they had been looking forward to a wedding and to grandchildren from the day they'd met Bruce. "I can die now," my mother had told me that Christmas, "knowing you're happy." She ran her fingers lightly across my back, my head resting in her lap. There was someone else in the world who could take care of me.

I wondered what they were doing, and pictured them sitting under the arbor my dad had built, smoking pot out of the hookah, maybe, and listening to the static-laced *Bob Dylan Hour* on the radio as dark clouds gathered, our three yellow Labs rolling in the muddy grass. Every time Bruce and I came for dinner I would have given anything to send Bruce away and stay the night in my mom's bed, eating Pop-Tarts and watching *Special Victims Unit* with her asleep in the bed beside me and her lumpy wool socks pressed against my leg, surrounded by velvet pillows and her incense smell, Dad's snores rising up from downstairs where he slept beside the woodstove. But instead I helped Bruce wash the dinner dishes, resenting his tiring, relentless displays of politeness, and then I'd hug them goodbye and climb in the cold car and drive the six minutes to our house in the woods, panicked with homesickness, like I was attending the world's longest sleepover. For years I'd lived across the country and hadn't felt a glimmer of desire to move back in with my family, not once.

When I reached the dock parking lot I could smell the lobster pound that was next door to my parents' house, and I swore I could hear the faint sounds of the Labs barking and my mom calling them inside, her wolf whistle carrying across the bay. The dock payphone had been disconnected, but I picked up the phone just in case and listened into it, then walked over to the hut where the sailing students took lessons. There were six pieces of rope that the students used to practice their knots, attached to a plank above a hitching post. Below each rope was the name of the knot the students were meant to tie—Bowline, Anchor Bend, Sheepshank, Halyard Hitch, Slip, and Reef. Sheepshank and Slip were still intact and I undid those and tried to redo them but the rope kept coming loose in my hands. I gave up and tied the pieces of rope together in pairs like children's shoelaces.

I wanted to walk down to the dock but someone was sitting on the end of the pier, hunched and small beside the few remaining rowboats. When she turned her head, I saw that it was Nancy.

Soon Bruce would be home, his lips purpled with wine, and we would share another bottle together and the squash I had stuffed with leftovers from another type of squash and rice dish and watch a video he had discovered at work of cats falling in slow motion and landing on their feet.

Though I felt shy I forced myself to walk down the ramp to the dock and sit on the opposite side of the pier from Nancy, slipping my feet, already cold and pruned from my wet sneakers, into the ocean because that's what I had envisioned I would do. I watched my feet in the freezing water, and after some sharp pain I couldn't feel them anymore. They looked fat and skittish, like they'd taken on a temperament of their own.

"Hey, stranger," she called from the other side of the pier. "I see you over there, pretending you don't see me." I wished I could hide myself from her. It felt important that she not recognize me, in the sickly, greenish light of an oncoming storm, my face caked with Sun-kissed Medium, but there was nowhere to go. She sat beside me and dangled her legs off the dock, her feet next to mine in the water like two smaller fish of the same species.

"I didn't want to bother you," I said, and she held out her hand to me, for a shake, I thought, but when she slipped her tiny, freezing hand into mine she just held it there like I might kiss it. She wore a man's overcoat, and a yellow, rubber rain hat. I couldn't tell looking at her that her brain had been altered in some grave, irreparable way. She was still a girl who would look good on the cover of a cereal box: upturned nose, freckles, blue eyes, quick to blush.

"I don't know if you remember me," I said. "I'm Mae, Roy and Becky's daughter."

"Of course I remember you," said Nancy. "I remember everything."

She took off her rain hat. Her white-blonde hair was braided in a crooked tangle down her back. "Do you know how to French braid? I've been trying on myself all summer." I started working on the knots. Her hair was brittle, as though salted by the sea. The nape of her neck was damp with sweat. Downy, dark hairs hid beneath the blonde. Hair didn't grow on the pink scar behind her left ear. The clouds had turned to purple and then to black, suspended above us. I pulled my feet from the water and waited for the painful circulation of blood. It was time to go, but Nancy had a lot of hair, and I was only halfway down her back.

One summer, a pack of teenagers, one of them Nancy, lit candles on the tennis court across the street from my parents' house, held hands, and spun each other in circles, sneakers squeaking as they whipped around faster and faster. Only after the kids left the tennis court did my dad go out and discover the courts littered with beer bottles and yellow wax, which would have to be cleaned by a professional. "Never be oblivious like that," my dad said when he returned home, shaking the dregs of their beers into our garden's slug traps.

But the next evening when the courts were clear and it was dark I snuck across the street and spun with the roller used for squeegeeing the courts dry, gripping the end of its long handle like a dance partner's hands, its weight a counterweight to my body, until I was queasy and had to lie down. The stars spiraled above me, and I pretended deliciously that I was sick and dizzy from beer and that everyone else was spinning in the surrounding darkness.

I tied off her braid, and tried to look her in the eyes. Looking her in the eyes felt like the next best thing to asking about her coma, which I didn't know how to do. When I got up to leave I reached out and balanced myself on her shoulders.

"Please don't go," she said. "If you stay I'll show you my best secret, as payback for the braid." She pulled a slimy sheet of seaweed from the water, smooth and alive, and draped it over the shoulders of my raincoat.

"I love your stole," she said. "Is that real mink?" By now Bruce would be home, calling my name. "Look, you're all dressed up now. Come out with me." The rowboats were unruly on the ends of their lines. She untied the smallest one and rooted the oarlocks out from a secret crevice.

"I can't," I said, but she climbed into the boat and patted the prow, the sun sinking behind her.

"If you don't come I'll have to row out to the island alone and that's just pathetic," she said. She dug in her pockets for a tin of sardines and a can of seltzer. "Dinner and drinks. Private island."

"I wish I could," I said. "I should get back to my boyfriend."

She began to drift out from the dock. "I'm supposed to wear a helmet all the time. Imagine what might happen without your company."

I climbed into her boat. When the rain began I took over rowing. The rain fell so hard all I could do was laugh. I rowed like a maniac, the oars flailing.

By the time we reached the island it was just light enough for me to follow Nancy's outline along the dark path to its center. Everything was giving off its growth smell in the rain.

"I just need a break," she said, lying down across the middle of the path. "Don't worry, this is normal."

"What should I do?" I said.

"Nothing. I get dizzy. It feels like I'll never stop spinning." I crouched beside her and held her hand, wondering if she was small enough that I could carry her. She pushed my hand away. "No dramatics," she said, rising. She leaned on me to walk. I watched the stream of stars where trees had been cleared for the pathway and tried to let them comfort me.

I had visited the island church when I was a little girl, but was still surprised to see its shape hidden in the overgrowth, one side of the steeple rotted away. Inside, the church smelled of raccoon droppings and death and beer. Clusters of bats hung from the rafters. Nancy flicked her lighter and let the flame play over bottles, scraps of newspaper, an acid-washed jean jacket. A tidy collection of sheep skulls lined the windowsill.

There was no chance of rowing back now, in the dark, in the rain, which was hammering against the roof and leaking in all around us. When I stepped toward Nancy a rivulet threaded down my neck.

"Tell me about this boyfriend," she said, interlocking her fingers with mine.

"Bruce is a good guy. A gentle giant."

"Bruce," she scoffed. "Does he hold doors open for old ladies?"

"He does. That's exactly right."

"Tell me about this thing you've got going with Bruce," she said. "Bruce. A fat person's name."

I felt sad for him. Bored and anguished and sad. Pressed against Nancy, my wet clothes were unbearably cold.

"I think he's my person," I said. Then, she kissed me. She didn't really want to know about Bruce. I kissed back. She was a bad kisser, frenzied and sloppy with too much tongue, and I didn't try my best either. We lay down on the floor of the church together, among the newspapers and soggy leaves and the threat of splinters from the rotting floorboards, and she climbed on top of me, the tip of her braid curled against my neck like a snake.

In my dreams I took lovers who were not Bruce, and always in the dream, before sex or after, I would feel a dawning dread. *There is someone I'm betraying*, I would think, the other lover still inside me, my fingers in their hair. I'd struggle to remember Bruce's name, dredging for the image of his good, round face, his thinning blond hair, his quick smile, the drooping eyelids that made him look sad and weary even as a little boy. He was always so hard to remember, but I always remembered him, and then I searched for him in mad remorse to confess, my guilt so fierce it turned the dream lucid. Each time waking up was glorious relief.

"Whoa there," Nancy said as though I were a bucking horse, "dizzy spell," and she lay down beside me, droplets of rain falling on her forehead, in my mouth, on the back of my hand. "You don't want this," she said. "I'm sorry. Tell Bruce I'm sorry. Tell him I'm the loneliest person in the world."

I had plans for the church. Bruce and I could scrub it clean and line the floor with colored pillows, hang lanterns from the ceiling and light candles in the eaves. We would have to keep the wedding small, so we could ferry guests out to the island. From the shore the parade of boats would look like a fisherman's funeral, and sympathizers would gather on the beach to wave, and the low-flying seaplane would tip its wings left and right in salute.

I just wanted to be that bride.

Acknowledgments

To Claudia Ballard, for your faith in me and in short stories, your impeccable intuition, your generosity and patience, thank you. Katie Raissian, extraordinary editor who knows my mind, it has been a joy to bring this book to life under your deeply insightful guidance. Elisabeth Schmitz, your brilliant eye missed nothing, and your connection to Maine and passionate vision made it immediately clear Grove Atlantic was my home.

Thank you to the entire Grove Atlantic team for championing this debut with such care, and special thanks to Morgan Entrekin, Deb Seager, and John Mark Boling. Thanks also to Amy Hundley, Julia Berner-Tobin, Charles Woods, and the art department. And to Chris Russell, for drawing the island of my dreams.

I'm enormously grateful to the editors who first published these stories: Jonathan Lee, Brigid Hughes, and the fantastic team at *A Public Space*; Amie Barrodale and Rocco Castoro at *Vice*; David Daley at *FiveChapters*; and Christine Cote at Shanti Arts Publishing.

To Harry Bauld, always. You treated me like a writer from the beginning, and that made all the difference.

Thank you to Chris Fink, for kind guidance and creative community. To early readers, writers, and friends from The

Putney School, Beloit College, and McSweeney's, thank you. You know who you are, and you got me through. Special thanks to Francesca Abbate, Scott Russell Sanders, Linda Gregerson, Kevin Link, and Jade Daugherty.

I owe so much to the Iowa Writers' Workshop. Deb West, Jan Zenisek, Kelly Smith, and Connie Brothers, you are saviors. Samantha Chang, Ethan Canin, Wells Tower, James Alan McPherson, and Marilynne Robinson, it was a gift to see your minds at work. Kevin Brockmeier and Charles Baxter, your teaching changed my life, and your ongoing support has helped me keep the faith.

For feeding me, dancing, making music, sharing your work and reading mine, thank you to so many workshoppers, and especially Ben Shattuck, Thessaly La Force, Daniel Cesca, Dina Nayeri, Devika Rege, Casey Walker, Stephen Narain, and Kiley McLaughlin (sister and mother of my heart). To Henry Finch, for everything. And to Thomas Gebremedhin, spot-on reader, advisor, healer.

To my Sorrento community and to my family, far and wide, your company has kept me grounded and given me joy. To Terry Noyes, remarkable uncle.

I will always be giving thanks for Sean Hershey, bosom friend and home base.

Finally, to my Dad and Kathleen, Mom and Bob. You've been with me every step of the way, believed in me, inspired me, and recognized me. I am so lucky to be your daughter. I love you all.